THE SECRET ZOO

THE FINAL FIGHT

Bryan Chick

Second Wish Press

This book is a work of fiction. References to real people, events, establishments, organizations, or locales, are intended only to provide a sense of authenticity, and are used to advance the fictional narrative. All other characters, and all incidents and dialogue, are drawn from the author's imagination and are not to be construed as real.

THE SECRET ZOO, THE FINAL FIGHT.
Copyright © 2017 by Bryan Chick
First Published in e-book form, 2017

Published by Second Wish Press

Cover art © 2017 Justin Gerard

For Ricky

THE STORM

Mr. Darby was in the Library of the Secret Society when the end began. He was standing by a towering bookcase, watching a monkey in a blue vest select a book from the top.

"No, no, that can't be the one!" he politely called out. "Look for the thick green spine!"

The monkey shrieked, partly out of irritation, it seemed, and then ran across a new shelf, his fingers grazing the books. He plucked one with a wide green spine, flipped through a few pages, and then put it back, having decided it wasn't the right one.

"*Mr. Darby!*" a voice rang out.

The old man turned and saw Solana running toward him from one of the eight entrances to the octagonal building. Behind her, the strings of beads across the doorway were still swaying. She had her quills out, her Descender gear ready. Something was wrong—a fact Mr. Darby knew before he saw the terror in her eyes.

He rushed toward Solana, the end of his long jacket stirring up colorful leaves that had fallen from the indoor trees. The commotion in the crowded library died, and Mr. Darby could feel the stares of all the patrons, animals and people alike. He stopped in front of Solana. "What is it?"

"I don't know!" She pointed to the doorway and added, "The sky!"

Mr. Darby quickly made his way out of the library and then suddenly stopped. Low, dark, swirling clouds seemed to be devouring the tops of buildings and trees like a monster made of fog, and deep shadows were falling across the city.

"What...what kind of storm is this?" Solana asked from beside him.

"It's not just a storm," Mr. Darby said. "It's DeGraff."

Solana flinched. Then she shook her head, as if unwilling to believe it.

The birds that couldn't get out from beneath the clouds began to fly in erratic paths and drop from the sky. On the crowded streets, animals and people recognized the danger and began to run for cover in the buildings.

Solana turned to go back into the library, but Mr. Darby grabbed her arm, stopping her. "The roof is made of glass," he said. Then he gestured toward the dark clouds and added, "It won't protect from that."

"Then where?" Solana asked.

The old man looked around and saw a nearby building

that seemed safe: the Institute of Light, a museum as old as the Secret Zoo. He touched the transmit button on his headset and, to the Crossers who were listening, said, "This storm is DeGraff's! Find cover—fast! Get to the Institute of Light if you can!" Then he turned his attention to the people and animals near him. "Everyone—follow us!"

Together, he and Solana led the charge away from the deadly looking storm front.

CHAPTER 1

IT'S IN THE BAG

3 Days Later

"Noah…*hurry*!"

Ella's voice was barely a whisper. Noah turned his attention to the object in his hand. A key. *The* key. The magic gold key that could open any lock. The key that a cheetah had once delivered to Noah's house in the middle of the night. The key that, in a way, had started this incredible, magical, and dizzying adventure with the Secret Zoo.

When Noah held the key to the jagged-edged slot in the door, it melted and slid into the lock. Then it solidified again. Noah turned his wrist. *Click!* The door was open.

"Go," Megan said.

Noah hesitated. He glanced over his shoulder and saw the playground of Clarksville Elementary—a weedy lawn partly blanketed in crisp autumn leaves. In the darkness, he could faintly make out the swings, the climbing walls, the basketball court. He'd lost count of how many times he and his friends had snuck into their school.

Ella brushed past Noah and pushed through the door. As she stepped inside, the other scouts followed—Megan,

4

Richie, and finally, Noah. The west wing of Clarksville Elementary was dimly lit by a few overhead lights. The four friends looked up and down the halls.

"All clear," Noah said.

His friends knew this meant it was safe to come out of their camouflage. Together, they opened the zippers on their Specter pants, prompting the chameleons on their bodies to crawl through the magic portals in their pockets and return to the Secret Zoo.

"The maintenance room?" Megan asked as she slowly became visible.

Noah turned to his year-younger sister and nodded. The maintenance room seemed the best place to start. It held the only entrance to the cellar—the abandoned dirt cellar from the old school that had once stood on the same grounds as the new Clarksville Elementary. If the rumors were true— the stories being passed around by excited voices in the halls and cafeteria—and tarantulas were really being spotted on the property, then the place to begin looking for them was the cellar, the room where DeGraff, the Shadowist, had once built a portal.

Noah checked the clock on a nearby wall: 7:26. All their parents, who'd gone out for dinner and a movie, wouldn't be home for at least two hours—the scouts had plenty of time. He led a cautious charge up the hall.

The scouts had other reasons to be worried. They hadn't

heard from Mr. Darby or the Descenders in three days. No messages from Marlo, no communications in their headsets, no late-night visits. It wasn't normal.

The four friends turned down a new hall and suddenly stopped. A noise, from one of the classrooms.

"What was that?" Richie whispered.

Noah held his finger to his lips and turned to his best friend, Richie, who was wearing his favorite stocking cap with the wide ribbed cuff and oversized pom-pom.

They stayed quiet and held their awkward poses, arms and legs stretched out at different angles. Everyone from the school should have gone home for the day. The scouts had seen the last car drive out of the parking lot twenty minutes ago—Mrs. Mathers, a fifth-grade teacher with bushy hair, weary eyes, and a permanent stack of papers under her arm.

But maybe something else was in Clarksville Elementary. Noah thought of all the visitors the Secret Zoo had brought to the school. Blizzard and Little Bighorn—a polar bear and a rhinoceros. Sasquatches. The Descenders and Specters. Even DeGraff, the feared enemy of the Secret Zoo.

"Probably the pipes," Noah said after a minute of silence had passed.

They headed out again, perhaps a little more quickly this time. Near the middle of a long hall was a room marked MAINTENANCE AND ELECTRICAL. Noah checked the

6

door—open—and pushed his way inside.

In the maintenance room, large boxy appliances steamed and spat. A web of pipes covered the ceiling and crossed the open spaces above. Noah glanced to one side of the room, where an old door was closed and sealed with a padlock. The cellar. He went to it and used his magic key. The shackle sprang from the steel body with such a loud *click!* that Richie jumped, sending the pom-pom on his hat into a dance.

"Ready?" Noah asked.

Megan answered with a quick nod that made her pigtails swing.

The door creaked as it opened, and a cool draft stroked Noah's skin. Darkness. Noah reached into the space and slid his hand along the wall until he found a light switch. A steep flight of concrete steps led to a dirt floor below. He remembered the last time the scouts had been here. DeGraff had hidden in one of the rooms and attacked them, capturing the Descenders.

Noah gathered what he could of his courage and walked onto the first step. Then he moved to the second, then the third. The smell of must and earth invaded his senses. He took the fourth step, the fifth, conscious of how closely his friends were following. He paused when he reached the dirt floor, and the scouts crowded around him. Just in front of the staircase was a hall, roughly six feet across and a hundred feet long. Both of the concrete walls had four carved-out sections—doorless entryways to other places. Light bulbs dangled from simple fixtures.

"No tarantulas," Richie said, taking a step back.

As he turned to go, Noah grabbed his arm. "We have to check," Noah said. "The rooms."

His friend opened his mouth to protest but then closed it. Two years of dealing with the Secret Zoo had taught Richie to be brave, at least a little. He'd come a long way from being the boy with a childish hat, shiny shoes, and a perpetual wedgie.

The scouts eased down the hall, looking through the entryways as they passed. Most of the rooms were empty, but one held an old furnace covered with dust. Noah's heart raced as he neared the entryway at the end of the hall—the passage that DeGraff had dragged the Descenders through to get to the portal in the back of the room. Noah took a deep breath. Then he turned and walked inside.

The room was empty, and the portal to the Secret Zoo that had once been in the far wall was still gone. There were no tarantulas, and no sign that any had been here.

"Nothing," Megan said.

"Good," Richie said. "Let's go—I hate this place."

Noah stared at the far wall, remembering the dark tunnel, and DeGraff dragging Solana into it. He imagined DeGraff's face: the two skull cavities where his nose should

8

have been, the bugs squirming in his flesh. DeGraff. A corpse kept alive by the magic in the shadows. A creature bent on taking over the Secret Zoo and destroying the world.

Noah felt a tug on his sleeve, and then he heard a voice, his sister's. "Noah, we should go."

Noah nodded, but he didn't move. He thought of the last time he'd seen DeGraff, eight days ago in the City of Species after the rescue of Tank and the Descenders. DeGraff had narrowly avoided capture, and then he'd escaped into the Creepy Critters sector, sealing its only passageway behind him.

"C'mon, Noah!"

His sister tugged so hard this time that he stumbled backward. He turned and followed the scouts out of the room, suddenly anxious to get away from his memories of this place. The friends charged up the hall and took the steps two at a time. Back in the maintenance room, Noah closed and locked the door.

"Let's get out of here," Ella said.

They fled the room and rushed down the hall, no longer concerned about being quiet. When they reached the glass wall of the media center, Megan and Ella stopped so suddenly that Noah and Richie practically fell over them. Something was crawling on the floor. Noah thought it was a rat, but then he saw the creature's eight legs and bulbous body. A tarantula. The spider froze in place. Then it quickly crawled through a gap beneath the front door of the media center.

"Guys," Ella said, "what do we do?"

Megan answered by holding her palm out to Noah, who dropped the magic key onto it. She walked to the entrance of the media center and opened the door. The scouts followed her into the room, which was softly lit by a few lamps.

"Where did it go?"

The scouts scanned the floor as they paced between the chest-high bookcases.

"It's gone," Megan said.

"How can it be *gone*?" Ella shot back.

Noah walked around the media specialist's desk. There was nothing beneath it but a pair of rubber boots that Ms. Anderson wore to go outside on rainy days.

"The books," Megan said. "Check the shelves."

"For *one* tarantula?" Ella said.

Megan shook her head. "No. For more."

Noah cringed at the thought, but he knew his sister was right. With the Secret Zoo, things rarely happened in moderation.

Noah squatted beside a bookcase and began to pull back the books to look behind them. Nothing. When he got to the end of the bookcase, he went to another, and another. Still nothing. He stood up straight and saw Richie's head pop up like a gopher's.

10

"Anything?" Noah asked.

Richie shook his head.

"Uhh…*guys*…"

Noah turned and saw Ella looking up. He followed her gaze. Dozens of tarantulas were crawling aimlessly along the ceiling.

Richie gasped and backed into a bookcase. Ella, her eyes wide, slowly shook her head.

"How did they get in here?" Megan asked.

"I have no idea," Noah said. "But we have to round them up."

"And put them *where*?"

Noah didn't have an answer. He touched the transmit button on the tiny headset in his ear and tried to contact the Descenders again: "Solana? Sam? Guys—it's Noah."

The other scouts stayed quiet as they listened to their own headsets. The four friends had worn them every day since the headsets had been given to them by the Descenders to secretly communicate back and forth.

"Guys?" Noah said, still touching his ear. "Tank? Anyone there?"

"Forget it," Megan said.

Noah looked up and saw the tarantulas again. Then he glanced around the room for something to put them in. Next to the checkout counter was a stack of book bags. As Noah ran to it, the other scouts followed.

"Here," he said as he tossed one to each of his friends.

"Book bags?" Richie said.

"Fill them up," Noah said. He held his book bag out to show that it had a Velcro strap that folded over the top. "That should keep them in."

"*Should?*" Richie said.

"You got a better idea?"

Richie thought about it for a few seconds and then shrugged.

Noah walked to a spot beneath the tarantulas and carefully climbed up a low bookcase, using the shelves as steps. The bookcase wobbled but didn't fall. He stood on the top and found that the ceiling was just out of reach.

"Throw me a book."

Megan tossed one up. Noah grabbed it out of the air and then held it so the spine was pressed flat against the ceiling. He held up the bag. When a tarantula crawled close enough, he used the book to sweep it into the bag.

"Go," he said to the other scouts. "Spread out."

Each of his friends grabbed a book, hurried off in a different direction, and climbed a bookcase. They walked along the tops, using their books the way Noah had. Tarantulas began to fill their bags. Megan jumped from her bookcase to another. She captured the two tarantulas overhead and then leaped to a new bookcase. Noah followed her lead. At his new location, he reached up and claimed

12

another tarantula. Then he jumped to a new spot.

Ella and Richie joined in, and for a few minutes, the scouts looked like frogs hopping across lily pads to stay out of the water. At one point, a tarantula fell off the ceiling and landed on Richie's head. Before Richie could panic, Noah jumped to the top of his best friend's bookcase, grabbed the tarantula with his free hand, and dropped it into his bag. Then he wiped his hand on his pants and tried to forget the way the big spider's hairy legs had felt against his skin.

Richie, his face pale with shock, simply said, "Thanks, man."

"No problem," Noah said. Then he jumped back to his bookcase, which teetered but didn't fall.

Before long—and after a couple more small mishaps—all the tarantulas were caught. The friends sealed their bags and climbed down to the ground.

"Now what?" Ella asked. When she held up her arm, Noah saw the tarantulas' bodies pushing against the side of her book bag. "You want to leave 'em in the drop box for Ms. Anderson to deal with?"

Noah imagined a second grader opening the book drop and then shrieking as a tarantula scurried out onto her Beverly Cleary book.

"The Secret Zoo," Noah said. "We have to take them back." He glanced at a nearby clock and added, "We have time."

As his friends thought about this, Noah saw several hairy legs curling out from a small opening in the top of his bag. He shook his arm and the tarantula dropped back down.

"Okay," Megan said. "Let's do it."

Noah nodded. Then he led the group out of the media center. In the halls, the scouts used the chameleons to camouflage themselves again. Seconds later, they pushed through the exit in the west wing, and Noah locked the door behind them. As they hurried onto Jenkins Street toward the Clarksville Zoo, Noah hoped they could make it to the Secret Zoo and back before their parents got home. And he hoped they wouldn't run into any more trouble.

CHAPTER 2

THE GATEWAY TO NO WAY

The scouts raced across the Clarksville Zoo, their book bags swinging at their hips. Though still camouflaged, they ran beneath trees and beside buildings to prevent their shadows from appearing in the moonlight. They'd decided to get into the Secret Zoo through the portal in Giraffic Jam, one of the easiest sectors to cross.

"Hello?" Megan said, and Noah realized she was trying her headset again. "Can anyone hear me?"

"Yeah," Richie said. "Me."

Noah glanced over and saw a tarantula slip out of his best friend's bag. The big spider tumbled across the sidewalk, then crawled into the grass.

"Watch it, Richie," Noah said as he scooped up the tarantula and put it into his bag. "You're dropping your loot."

The friends reached Giraffic Jam, the giraffe exhibit at the Clarksville Zoo. The building was several stories tall, covered with ivy, and capped with a dome roof. Noah checked the front door—locked—and then used his magic key to get inside. The scouts came out of their camouflage as they charged up a short flight of stairs and then stepped onto a wooden deck. More than ten feet off the ground, this deck circled the inside of the building, providing a place for visitors to feed the giraffes. Not a single animal was in sight.

"Where are the giraffes?" Richie asked.

Megan pointed to a large square opening in the ground—the passage that led to the Secret Giraffic Jam. In the hole, which was normally covered by a movable platform, a steep ramp disappeared into darkness. "And why is that open?"

"Hold on, guys," Noah said as he slowed to a stop. "I don't like the looks of this."

The scouts stood still and glanced around the exhibit. A small waterfall provided the only movement and sound.

"What do we do?" Megan asked.

"I say we dump the tarantulas and get the heck out of here!" Richie said.

Noah shook his head and stared at the dark, open passage. "No way. Something's wrong, and we need to find out what it is."

"He's right," Ella said.

She walked across the deck, crawled over the railing, and jump-dropped to the grass. Her friends followed in exact fashion, careful not to tip their bags. They ran across the exhibit and took the ramp into the ground, which led to a section of the Grottoes, a magical system of tunnels that

16

connected to the Secret Zoo and distant exhibits of the Clarksville Zoo. The familiar tunnel had four passages, each covered with a velvet curtain, and the scouts took the one marked THE SECRET GIRAFFIC JAM.

As Noah stepped into the sector, moist air struck him. The Secret Giraffic Jam was dark, and not because it was night in the Secret Zoo—a thick fog was blocking the light, which normally came from fixtures mounted to the walls.

"What's going on?" Ella asked.

Noah had no idea. He'd never seen fog as thick as this in the Secret Zoo. The web of winding walkways that stretched skyward—the prominent characteristic of the Secret Giraffic Jam—was barely visible. In fact, Noah could hardly see more than thirty feet in any direction.

The better part of Noah wanted to turn and run. But he forced himself to touch the transmit button on his headset and say, "Hello? Anyone there?"

The scouts listened and waited.

"Sam?" Noah added. "Solana?"

Seconds passed. Noah felt the cool fog invading his lungs with each inward breath.

"No one's here," Megan said. "The City of Species?"

"Maybe," Noah said. "The radio waves can't reach the city because it's beyond another portal. Should we keep going?"

"No," Megan said. "We need to get home. Mom and

Dad will be—"

To their left, a branch suddenly broke. And then several more. Noah heard fallen leaves being trampled.

"Sam?" Ella said, her voice sounding hopeful.

In the place they were looking, the fog began to swirl and break apart. Five giraffes slowly appeared, and it took only a few seconds for Noah to realize something was different about them. Their muscles bulged, their horns were longer, and patches of their fur had fallen out. Their eyes were tinted red, as if something wicked was growing inside them, and Noah realized that something was. DeGraff's magic. The scouts had seen it before: the sasquatches, the animals in Creepy Critters, Charlie Red—all had been changed by the Shadowist. The giraffes stopped in front of the scouts, and as they lowered their long necks, Noah held his arms out to his sides and forced his friends to take a step back.

A giraffe moved its head forward, stopping just inches from Noah's face. Its ears were crooked and bent, its nostrils crusted with snot. Its long tongue slipped out and lapped the air, just missing Noah, who winced at the creature's rancid breath.

The other giraffes began to lean in, looking ready to chomp and bite.

"Guys..." Noah half whispered. "Turn and run. Take out the portal by tearing down the curtain. But first, follow

18

my lead."

"Your lead?" Richie asked. "What are—"

Noah suddenly swung his arm, slamming his book bag against the giraffe's head. The Velcro straps popped open and tarantulas poured out. Some tumbled to the ground, but others caught onto the giraffe and started crawling along its fur. The giraffe whipped its long neck, flinging the spiders everywhere.

"Now!" Noah hollered.

His friends attacked and their book bags connected. Tarantulas flew in all directions, like confetti from a nightmare.

Noah turned and practically dove through the portal, his friends following. "The curtain—grab and pull!" he said, recalling how much force it had taken to break the curtain rings in the portal beneath Gator Falls.

The scouts grabbed the curtain and pulled. Nothing happened. Noah looked up. Six rings were all that kept it up.

"Harder!"

His friends planted their heels and leaned back, their hands gripping the velvet. The giraffes—or the things that had once been giraffes—closed in.

The rings rattled and moved, but they didn't snap free. Noah turned, hoisted part of the curtain over his shoulder, and plowed forward. Nothing.

"Forget it!" Noah said. "Run!"

As the scouts took off in the Grottoes, the giraffes followed, their heads nearly dragging along the ceiling. The scouts charged up the ramp. In Giraffic Jam, they climbed onto the deck and ran across the winding platform, a place the giraffes couldn't follow. They soon pushed through the exit of the building and came to a quick halt just a few feet down the outdoor sidewalk. Three people were standing in their path—security guards from the zoo.

"It's us," Ella said, knowing that everyone at the Clarksville Zoo recognized the scouts.

The guards stayed quiet. A burly man with round cheeks rolled a toothpick across his lips and then slowly chewed on one end. He ran his fingers through his messy hair and scratched his chin.

"You need to close Giraffic Jam!" Megan said. "The giraffes are under DeGraff's spell! You need—"

"And we found tarantulas in our school!" Ella cut in. "They were—"

"The portal!" Richie interrupted. "We had to—"

"Slow down!" the guard with the toothpick said. "One at a time!"

Megan told the guards everything: the tarantulas, their school, what had just happened in Giraffic Jam. The guards listened, but in a disinterested way. The big guard continued to roll the toothpick across his lips.

"That it?" a guard asked when Megan was finished.

20

Megan nodded.

The guards glanced at one another. Then the big guard took a step forward and a slant of moonlight fell across his face, revealing a long cut on his cheek, a near-open wound with a wet scab. Noah suddenly realized the man's hair was messy because clumps had fallen out. The guard unholstered his baton and let it dangle by his leg. He smiled, and Noah flinched at what he saw. A few of his teeth were pointed. Fangs.

DeGraff had gotten to the guards with his magic.

"Don't," Noah said. "Leave us...leave us alone." He glanced around. The dark zoo landscape was creepier than ever—full of hiding places and dead ends. How many other guards and animals had DeGraff infected?

"What do we do with them?" one of the guards asked.

In answer, the guard smacked his baton against his open palm. Noah looked back and thought about the monstrous giraffes in the exhibit. There was no place for the scouts to run and hide.

Hide. An idea struck him.

"Guys," he whispered to his friends, "ghost it. Now."

The scouts acted at once, each unzipping a pocket on their Specter pants. Chameleons crawled onto their bodies, quickly blending them into their surroundings.

"*Get 'em!*" a guard hollered.

The men charged, batons swinging, but the scouts had

already ducked out of the way. They ran across the lawn, landing on their toes to minimize their footprints in the grass—a Specter trick.

"Which way did they go?" a guard called out.

"I don't know!" a second guard answered.

Though the scouts couldn't see one another, they had no problem moving in a pack. Noah could tell where his friends were by their breathing, their body heat, and their quiet steps. They ran to the far side of a souvenir shop, stopped running, and listened. Noah peered around the edge of the building. Giraffic Jam was at least a hundred feet away now, partly hidden by a few tall trees and bushes that hadn't yet lost their leaves. The guards were still standing on the sidewalk, glancing in all directions, their batons held out to their sides. For a quick moment, they looked like the bumbling Keystone Cops Noah had seen in old black-and-white movies. One of the guards seemed to see something—movement in the distance. Then he hollered, "This way!" and the guards ran off, disappearing behind the zoo carousel.

"They're gone," Richie said, and when Noah heard his voice, he realized his friend was standing right beside him.

"There might be more," said Megan. "They're not—"

A long, slow growl came from behind the scouts. Noah didn't move. He smelled the breath of an animal—a warm cloud drifting over the scouts. The animal's breath had a familiar odor, and when Noah placed it, he turned around to see a massive polar bear with a blocky head and paws the size of catcher's mitts.

"Blizzard?" Noah said, his voice a half question of surprise. He didn't know if Blizzard had come from the Secret Zoo or his exhibit.

"He's okay!" Ella said, and Noah saw the bear's fur being pressed down as Ella stroked his side. "DeGraff's magic—it hasn't gotten to him."

"But it might," Noah said. "We have to get him out of here."

"How?" Richie asked.

"We'll ghost him," Noah said. "And I know a place he can hide."

When no one opposed this idea, Blizzard growled and lowered his stomach to the ground. His intention for the scouts was obvious: *Get on.* Megan claimed the front spot just behind Blizzard's neck, and then Ella and Richie climbed on. Noah took the final seat.

"Okay," Noah said, "ghost him."

The scouts opened the left pockets on their Specter pants, calling dozens of chameleons to crawl onto Blizzard. Parts of the big bear seemed to turn invisible—his head, his legs, areas along his massive sides. Within seconds, he was as hidden as the scouts.

"Go!" Noah called out as he swatted Blizzard's hind leg.

The polar bear rose and then charged across the lawn. He ran up a flight of stairs and slowed down as he emerged on a different side of the zoo.

"My house!" Noah said. "Get us out of here!"

Blizzard swung his long neck to look both ways, and then turned onto a concrete path—a path, Noah knew, that offered a quick route to a private exit along one wall of the zoo. They passed PizZOOria and Creepy Critters, buildings whose features were seemingly wiped out by the darkness. Noah bounced around as Blizzard's hefty paws thudded along.

Blizzard cut onto the grass to take a shortcut and veered around a fountain with a bronze statue of a porpoising penguin. He trampled through the crinkly remains of a summer flower bed, then lengthened his strides, the scouts clinging to one another to keep from falling off.

The exit appeared—a weighty wrought-iron gate with statues of small birds seemingly perched across the top. Blizzard headed straight for it and didn't bother to slow down. The gate broke off its hinges and flew like a giant Frisbee before landing in a grassy ditch.

"Stay close to the wall!" Noah called out to Blizzard.

Blizzard grunted to show he understood. Then he ran along the perimeter of the zoo behind the wooded backyards of Noah's neighbors. Noah glanced over his shoulder. It looked like they weren't being followed, but he couldn't tell what might be hiding in the shadows.

CHAPTER 3

A PREVIOUS PORTAL

As the scouts led Blizzard across Noah's backyard, a private place surrounded by tall trees, they opened the right pockets in their Specter pants and came out of their camouflage like figures from a fog. Blizzard made his way past Fort Scout, branches snapping beneath his paws, and then kicked through a windblown pile of fallen leaves. A shed sat in the back corner of Noah's yard, partly concealed by overgrown shrubs and the low limbs of a few trees. Noah walked to it and quietly opened the double doors. The space was crowded with tools, boxes, and ceramic pots. The scouts went inside and pushed things around to make room. Then they stepped back into the yard. Blizzard, knowing what to do, walked into the shed, the floor creaking and groaning beneath his weight. Then he found enough space to turn around and face the front.

"This is all we got," Noah said. He reached in and patted Blizzard's head.

"Guys…what's going on?" Richie asked.

"Let's check from Fort Scout." Noah briefly turned his attention back to Blizzard, saying, "Bliz, you'll be safe here until we can figure things out. We have to go right now, but we'll check on you."

The big bear lowered his head and grunted.

Noah touched Blizzard a final time and then closed the shed doors. The friends headed across the yard and climbed into their tree fort. Megan found the binoculars and looked out across the Clarksville Zoo.

"See anything?" Noah asked.

Instead of answering, Megan handed over the binoculars. Noah positioned the lenses before his eyes and stared out. Most of the lights at the zoo were still off. Noah could see some things—the silhouettes of Metr-APE-olis, the Wotter Park, and the Forest of Flight—but it was too dark to make out much detail. He tried to locate the animals and couldn't. Then he gave the binoculars to Ella, who took a turn looking before handing them over to Richie.

Noah tried to figure out what was going on. He thought of the fog, the giraffes, and the way the scouts couldn't contact the Descenders with their headsets. "DeGraff is taking over the zoos—the Clarksville Zoo *and* the Secret Zoo."

The scouts traded uneasy glances, and it was clear to Noah that they agreed.

Noah headed for the spiral staircase, saying, "Let's talk inside."

They made their way out of the tree fort and into the

house. Noah checked the clock—they still had a half hour before his parents got home. In the living room, they dropped onto the couch and chairs, exhausted. Megan said, "What do we do?"

Noah thought about the Descenders, the Specters, Mr. Darby, their animal friends. No one was here to help.

"Should we tell our parents?" Megan asked. "The police?"

Noah wondered what it would mean to expose the Secret Zoo. And the magic—it would no longer be safe. "I don't know. Maybe we should—"

He glanced up the staircase to his bedroom. He'd heard something—a board creaking.

"I heard it, too," Richie said, having noticed Noah's interest.

Noah glanced at Ella and Megan. He could tell by their wide eyes that they'd heard the same thing. Another board creaked, louder this time.

"Someone's up there," Ella said.

Megan suddenly jumped to her feet and headed for the staircase with quick, cautious strides.

"Meg, wait!" Noah whispered. But he was already off the couch and following his sister, along with Ella and Richie.

As the four of them slowly headed up the staircase, something clunked in Noah's room. The scouts paused, traded worried looks, then finished making their way up the stairs. They gathered around Noah's open bedroom door and listened. Another board creaked, and Noah realized the sounds were coming from his walk-in closet. He instantly recalled what had happened in there just days ago: the portal, Charlie Red, the monkeys. Noah had been attacked.

The room was quiet and dark. As the scouts cautiously stepped inside, they saw a silhouette near the closet doorway. A man—a lanky man whose hair was standing straight up. Ella gasped and grabbed Noah's arm. The man walked over to Noah's desk and turned on the lamp, revealing that he was actually a teenage boy. He had a crooked Mohawk and round goggles with tinted lenses and a wide rubber strap. He wore filthy blue overalls and a T-shirt that had once been white. The scouts had met him before.

"Zak?" Noah said. Zak belonged to the Teknikals, a group of geniuses who built machines from mechanics and magic. "What are you... How did you..."

"Your parents home?" Zak asked.

Noah shook his head.

"Don't freak, bro," Zak said. "At least not until you see who I brought with me."

More noises came from Noah's closet. Then an old man with a long gray beard and a flowing velvet jacket stepped out into the room. Mr. Darby. He stood up straight and nodded at the scouts as he used his palm to sweep dust off his jacket.

The closet floorboards creaked again. Then a young teenager stepped out. He wore a black leather jacket, and his long bangs dangled in his eyes. Sam, the leader of the Descenders who safeguarded the perimeter of the Clarksville Zoo.

Sam said, "Noah, what's the best way out of here?"

"Out of where?"

"Your *house*," Sam said, as if this should have been obvious. "This *is* your house, right?"

Noah nodded.

"Then how do you get out of it?" He looked around again, and then motioned at the window. "This?"

Noah shook his head and pointed to the hallway. "The front door is downstairs."

As Sam headed that way, he said, "I'll dispatch the troops. We'll set up a perimeter and bring down the gateways at the zoo."

"All of them," Mr. Darby said. "Block all access to our world."

"*What?*" Noah said. "Close the portals? What are you *talking* about?"

"Drastic measures for dire circumstances—I can't avoid it."

"But you can't close the portals!" Ella said.

More noises in the closet, and then a young teenage girl

stepped out. She had wild blond hair clipped to different lengths, wore purple leather boots that stopped near her knees, and was chomping a piece of gum. Hannah. She casually nodded at the scouts and then followed Sam out into the hall and down the stairs.

Noah turned his attention to the closet. From his angle, he couldn't see into it. "How…"

Zak said, "Remember the velvet curtain that Charlie Red used to get into your closet? The one that you gave to us?"

"Of course," Noah said.

"Your coordinates were still locked in. Me and a group of Tekkies were able to reengineer it."

Mr. Darby looked at Zak and said, "Most resourceful, these young men."

Though Noah couldn't see into his closet, he knew what was now at the back of it—a velvet curtain attached above a large hole in the wall where the heating vent had been.

Something small shot out of the closet. A bright blue bird flew around the room and then landed on Noah's shoulder. Marlo.

Noah positioned his head for the best view of the kingfisher. "You okay?"

Marlo chirped once to show that he was.

Noah turned to Mr. Darby and said, "The other animals—are they all right?"

"Some," the old man said. "But things are very uncertain at this point."

Another person walked out of the closet—an attractive girl with long dark hair that looped her ears and trailed down her back. She wore a blue leather jacket and fingerless gloves—gloves, Noah knew, that could sprout ten-inch quills. Solana. She winked at Noah and ran into the hall, followed by three Descenders Noah didn't recognize.

A big man with a shiny bald head and mounded muscles stepped into the room. Tank. When he got close to Noah, he held his massive fist out toward him, and Noah lightly fist-bumped Tank's walnut-sized knuckles.

Six new Descenders came out of the walk-in closet, one after another. Two Specters, Elakshi and Lee-Lee, appeared. They nodded at the scouts as they headed into the hall. Noah went to the window and looked out. Keeping to the shadows, the Secret Cityzens were heading off in different directions.

"Has he taken over the Clarksville Zoo?" Mr. Darby asked.

"Huh?" said Noah.

"The animals—has DeGraff gotten to them with his magic?"

Noah told Mr. Darby about the giraffes.

"And the security guards?"

Noah nodded.

"That means the sectors are his, too. Most, at least."

32

The scouts told Mr. Darby about the tarantulas at their school. Looking worried, the old man simply listened.

"How did this happen?" Richie asked.

"A storm," Mr. Darby said. "DeGraff conjured a storm to infect us with his dark magic."

"Is the City of Species safe?"

Mr. Darby shook his head. He gestured to the Descenders still coming from Noah's closet, saying, "We managed to escape into the basement of an old museum in the City of Species, the Institute of Light. Some animals did, too—Gifteds, mostly." He motioned to Zak and added, "Our young friend had a brilliant idea. The curtain that once opened to your room was being kept in the museum. He did some work with it, and hung it in the basement. Now"—Mr. Darby gestured around him—"here we are. And now we must close the portals to your world before DeGraff and his growing army can use them."

"But why not fight?" Megan asked. "The Descenders can track down DeGraff and—"

"The storm's dark magic is too powerful. Our Descenders would only become DeGraff's minions if they stayed in the shadows of the clouds for long."

Noah looked at the closet again. A man with a shaggy beard stepped into his room, and then a woman with short spiked hair. Noah watched them pass. Then he took a few steps forward, and on his shoulder, Marlo chirped, as if warning Noah to be careful. Noah peered into the long narrow closet and saw a curtain the size of a beach towel dangling along the wall. Crushed drywall lay beneath it. As Noah watched, the curtain bulged outward and then slipped off the body of a teenage boy in a hooded jacket. The teenager brushed past Noah on his way out of the room. Then Evie, the leader of the Specters, appeared.

Noah backed away from the scene, which was suddenly too much to believe. The portals, the magic, the Secret Zoo. A polar bear was sleeping in his shed, and people were entering his world through a portal in his closet.

"Mr. Darby!"

Noah flinched at the voice, which had come directly into his ear. Sam was talking over the radio waves everyone shared. "We got a problem. We're at the Clarksville Zoo. The gateways…we can't close them!"

Mr. Darby touched the transmit button on his earpiece and said, "What do you mean you can't—"

"The curtains won't come down!"

"How many have you tried?"

"Four. Five, maybe."

Mr. Darby seemed to think about this. He shared a look with Noah, Tank, and a few Descenders. "Keep trying. Go to every one, and do it quickly."

"Yes, sir," Sam said, and then the radio waves went silent.

"We had the same problem!" Megan said. "At Giraffic Jam!"

Mr. Darby raised an eyebrow and stared at Megan. "Then DeGraff has done something to cause this," he said. "He altered their magic." Mr. Darby stared at a spot on the floor. Then he said, "Sam, get back to Noah's. The rest of you—I want you to surround the Clarksville Zoo. If you can't bring down the portals, stay and guard them. If you see anything, let us know immediately."

"Roger," Sam said. Then, to the Descenders, he added, "Everyone—we clear?"

A few Descenders responded that they were. Then the radio waves went silent again.

Noah shook his head, barely able to believe all the things going on around him. Descenders were surrounding the Clarksville Zoo, where the portals were being kept open by the Shadowist. Fear washed over Noah as he realized the Secret Zoo was going to war—and it was doing so in his neighborhood.

*

"Are you sure about this?" Noah asked.

Mr. Darby raised an eyebrow over his dark sunglasses. "No. Not at all. But I'm at a loss, Noah—you must understand that."

Noah nodded. Then he glanced at the clock on his desk. His parents wouldn't be home for at least another twenty minutes.

The Secret Cityzens had stopped coming through the portal, and the only people in the house other than the scouts were Mr. Darby, Tank, Evie, Zak, and Sam, who'd come back inside. Marlo was still perched on Noah's shoulder. Mr. Darby had just shared his idea for keeping the scouts safe. He wanted to post someone at each of their houses.

"DeGraff could attack your world at any moment," Mr. Darby said. "My first priority is your protection."

Noah glanced at Sam, the person Mr. Darby had ordered to stay at Megan and Noah's. "Sam can stay in my closet," he said. "And he can step into the portal if he needs to hide."

"And Evie's coming to my house?" Ella asked.

Evie looked out from behind her long bangs with one eye and softly nodded.

"It shouldn't be too hard to conceal her from your mother," Mr. Darby said, referring to the Specter's power to camouflage. Then he looked at Richie and added, "Are you comfortable with Tank staying with you?"

Richie nodded.

"Is there a place he can hide from your parents, if needed?"

"Yeah," Richie said. "My room. It's really *that* messy."

Mr. Darby walked toward the middle of the group, saying, "Okay, it's decided, then. I'll head back to the City of Species with Zak—the Teknikals have work to do."

"On what?" Noah asked.

"Our best hope for stopping the animals from invading your world," Mr. Darby said. "I'll explain later. Zak—come with me."

As the pair began to walk toward the closet, Noah said, "What about the portal in my room?"

"It opens to the Institute of Light. We'll keep it guarded." Mr. Darby took a few more steps and then added, "Use your headsets to communicate, but remember...the airwaves can't pass through the portals."

Noah nodded. "If we need to tell you something, I'll send a note with Marlo."

Mr. Darby paused at the open doorway to the closet and looked back at the scouts. "If nothing happens tonight, see if you can find out how those tarantulas got into your school. A portal, maybe? It might mean DeGraff is using his new powers to open secret gateways to more places."

Noah nodded.

"If you find a portal, try to take it down." Mr. Darby turned to leave, and Ella called out his name. The old man looked back, saying, "Yes?"

"Our friends...Podgy and Little Bighorn...all the others. Are they safe?"

Mr. Darby frowned. "I don't know, Ella. They're not in the Institute of Light, and I don't know how much of the

Secret Zoo is now under DeGraff's control."

"But they could be safe somewhere else, right?" Richie said. "A building? Another basement?"

"Yes," Mr. Darby said. "But let's not make that our concern now. We have the world to consider—yours and ours."

The room went quiet, and the scouts traded worried glances.

"This is it," Mr. Darby said in a heavy voice. "The final fight."

CHAPTER 4

SECRET SLEEPOVERS

Tank walked into Richie's oversized closet and began clearing a spot on the floor.

"You're not thinking about building another portal, are you?" Richie asked.

Tank looked at Richie, realized he was joking, and went back to work, saying, "Give me a hand. Your parents could be home any—" He picked up a white toy robot with blue markings. "What the heck is this?"

"R2-D2."

"Are too *what* do?"

"*Star Wars*, you know." Then Richie realized Tank *didn't* know. He slowly shook his head, saying, "You really miss out on some stuff."

Tank raised one eyebrow, seemed to consider this, and then tossed R2-D2 into the corner.

Richie helped move things around, and before long, a spot was clear. Tank took a seat, his back against the wall. Richie did the same opposite him.

"Will your parents come in?" Tank asked.

"Not without knocking," Richie said. He stared at

Tank—his bald head, his broad shoulders, the web of scars on his hands. "You're in my *room*," Richie said. "Do you have any idea how weird that is?"

Tank nodded. As he looked around the closet, Richie followed his gaze: stacks of clothes, board games, old toys and electrical gadgets. "So this is Richie's life?"

"Yeah. Sort of."

Tank smiled. "Being a kid is good to you, huh?"

Richie shrugged. "Sometimes. Sometimes Wide Walt puts me in a locker."

"Who? That bully at your school?"

Richie nodded and looked at his feet to avoid Tank's gaze. "But other than that, it's pretty good. I have Noah. He's my best friend."

Tank smiled. "Yeah. I kind of noticed."

"Is Mr. Darby yours?"

"Mr. D? I guess so. He's best friend to a lot of people. Animals, too."

The two became quiet. Richie remembered the security guards in the Clarksville Zoo—what DeGraff's magic had done to them. Then he pictured the giraffes.

"Tank," he said, "I'm scared."

Richie, expecting to be told not to worry, flinched when Tank said, "I am, too, bub."

The front door to the house creaked open and Richie could hear his mother whispering to his father. He quickly got out of the closet, turned off the lights, and crawled into bed with his Specter pants still on.

"Try to sleep some, kid," Tank whispered.

"Will you?"

"Not likely."

Richie realized something. The Descenders, Tank—they sometimes went days without sleeping.

"See you tomorrow," Tank added. "If not sooner."

And Richie, knowing what that meant—knowing that DeGraff's army could strike at any moment—closed his eyes and worried about what the rest of the night would bring.

*

"Evie..." Ella said. She looked around her bedroom, adding, "Where are you?"

Over by the dresser, Evie seemed to take form—her arms, her legs, her black boots. That meant her chameleons were crawling into her pocket. Once the last chameleon was gone, Evie appeared fully. She crossed her arms and looked around at Ella's pink bedsheets, pink pillows, and pink drapes.

"Cool, right?" Ella asked.

Evie shrugged. "Pink. Where's my spot if I need to sleep?"

Ella realized how messy things were. She walked beside her bed and kicked through the stuff on the floor—clothes, cleats, her grass-stained soccer uniform. After a few seconds, a space opened on the carpet. She went to her closet, grabbed her sleeping bag (pink), and unrolled it on the floor. "Ta-da."

Evie nodded. Then she stood by the window and asked, "Can you see the zoo from here?"

"No," Ella said. "My house is too far back."

Evie looked in one direction, then another. To Ella, it seemed like she was scanning her neighbors' yards. Maybe she was looking for the tarsiers, the zoo animals that hid in the trees.

"Things will happen quickly now," Evie said. "The animals—they'll march across your world."

"Not if we stop DeGraff," Ella said.

"Stop?"

"Kill," Ella said, not liking the word even though it was the right one.

"How do you kill someone who's already dead?"

Ella had wondered the same thing—all the scouts had. They'd seen DeGraff up close—his empty eye sockets and decaying flesh. DeGraff was more than a hundred years old, kept from death by a dark magic.

Silence. After almost a minute, Evie asked, "What's it like?"

"What's what like?"

"Your world."

Ella shrugged even though Evie was still looking out

the window and couldn't see her. "Not so bad. We have problems, I guess."

"Is it worth dying for?"

"Huh?"

"Your world," Evie said. "Is it worth dying for?"

"I…." Ella couldn't think of a thing to say.

"You may need to," Evie said. "We all might."

Ella still wanted to say something, but words felt impossible.

Evie turned to Ella and frowned. "You should call your friends. Tell them to leave their Specter pants on in case the fight begins tonight."

Ella thought of her friends, her family, and how badly she wanted to keep everyone safe. Then she reached up and touched the transmit button on her earpiece.

*

"You leaving those on?" Sam asked.

"Huh?" Noah said.

Sam gestured to the Specter pants Noah was wearing.

"Oh," Noah said as he glanced down at his legs. Ella had just given the scouts instructions to wear their Specter pants to bed. "Yeah. What's wrong with that?"

Sam shrugged. "Nothing, I guess."

"You *guess*?"

"I just have a problem with the way Specters do things. They hide. Descenders fight."

"I've seen Specters fight," Noah said. In Creepy Critters, he'd used the chameleons to build a mirage to hide the portal to the City of Species and nearly trapped DeGraff, who'd escaped into the shadows at the last moment. "Besides, I'm going to do whatever I can to protect myself, and it's not like we have a spare set of Descender gear lying around."

"I wouldn't be so sure of that." Sam tipped his head toward the closet. "The portal. Tameron's in the Institute of Light. He's still injured from when DeGraff held us prisoner, and that frees up his gear."

Tameron's backpack contained a powerful tail that could smash through concrete walls and thick panes of glass. In the Secret Creepy Critters, Ella had used his tail to fight off the Shadowist.

"DeGraff's coming for your world," Sam said. "Do you want to hide or fight?"

Noah thought of all the times he'd fled from his problems. Charlie Red, the sasquatches, DeGraff, even Wide Walt, the bully at his school. How often had Noah *not* fought back?

"Leave 'em on, if you want," Sam said. "But let's go get Tameron's gear."

Noah looked at his pants again. Wouldn't it be easier to be a Specter and just fade away? "I don't know…"

"C'mon," Sam said, and he took a step toward the

closet. "The Institute of Light—it's just over there."

Noah looked toward Megan's room. "What if something happens while we're gone? What if DeGraff attacks?"

"We'll be gone fifteen minutes—thirty minutes at the most."

A Descender. Someone who ignored the rules and lived by his own code. What would it be like to fight back against Charlie Red and DeGraff's growing army? What would it be like to win?

"Wait a minute," Noah said. He scooped up a wad of dirty clothes from his floor and stuffed it under the covers of his bed.

"What are you doing?" Sam asked.

Noah opened a pocket on his Specter pants and chameleons crawled out, one after another, their bodies filled with the magic of the Secret Zoo. They made their way onto the mattress and spread out along the pile of clothes. Noah shut his pocket once twenty chameleons were out, enough for what he wanted to do.

He closed his eyes and took a deep breath. He concentrated on controlling the chameleons with his thoughts, just like he had in Creepy Critters. He imagined himself lying on his bed. What would his body look like beneath the covers? How would his head rest on his pillow? Would his lips be closed or parted?

He opened his eyes and witnessed the magic of the Secret Zoo. The chameleons had made his wad of clothes look exactly like him—Noah in bed, a dull expression on his face. A perfect mirage of Noah sleeping.

"Nice," Sam said. "Good thinking."

The real Noah smiled, proud of his achievement.

Marlo sprang from his perch on the windowsill and touched down on Noah's shoulder. He glanced from Noah to the image on the bed, looking a bit confused.

Noah took a step toward the closet. It felt good to be decisive. Marlo chirped, as if to show support. Or maybe concern.

Sam nodded. Then he turned and led Noah toward the Institute of Light.

On his way, Noah saw his red hunting cap on the dresser. As he reached for it, he remembered how Solana sometimes teased him about the hat being childish. And it was, Noah thought. It made him look like a little kid.

He grabbed the hat, considered it for a few seconds, and then tossed it back on the dresser. Then, as he walked into the closet, he stuffed his hands in his jacket pockets the way the Descenders often did.

CHAPTER 5

BACK FOR THE PACK

As the gateway curtain slipped down Noah's back, he entered a large room with a tall ceiling and concrete walls—the basement of the Institute of Light. The area was stocked with boxes and framed artwork. Bronze statues of people and animals were neatly organized on wire shelves, tags tied to their wrists and wings and flippers. As many as twenty people were there, many of them sitting on the floor, their backs against the walls. Descenders. Noah guessed they'd stayed back to protect one another and the Secret Zoo. A few were standing by the doorways, on guard and tense.

Animals also crowded the room. Among them, Noah saw a lion, an ostrich, a koala, and a bear with her two cubs. Dozens of prairie dogs were crawling around, sniffing the floor and sitting up on their haunches. P-Dog was among them, and when he saw Noah, he hurried over and moved his front legs up Noah's shin. Noah said, "P-Dog, you're okay!" and patted the prairie dog's head. Then he glanced around for more of his animal friends—Little Bighorn, Podgy, Louie, Ko—but didn't see any.

"How long will this place be safe?" Noah asked.

Sam shrugged. "A week, a day, an hour. DeGraff could hit us at any moment. We don't know his plan."

Small spots of light dotted the air, blinking on and off. Fireflies, as many as fifty. Noah didn't understand what they were doing in the basement of the museum, but it seemed normal enough for the Secret Zoo.

A teenage boy was sitting with his back to the wall. His leg, which was in a cast, was stretched out in front of him. He wore a tight knit cap with a short brim that partly masked his eyes. A large canvas bag was propped up against him. Tameron. The Descender met Noah's gaze.

Noah rushed over and kneeled beside Tameron. He looked at the cast and asked, "Does it hurt?"

Tameron shook his head. "Nah, man. Just stops me from being who I'm supposed to be."

Noah knew what he meant. A Descender.

Sam walked over and nodded at Tameron's backpack, saying, "How about we give Noah a chance?"

Tameron tipped his head back so he could clearly see out from beneath the low brim of his cap. He stared at Noah and said, "You think you're ready?"

Noah glanced around the room at the other Descenders. They were watching, waiting to hear his answer. Even Marlo, who was still on Noah's shoulder, seemed anxious to hear what Noah was going to say.

"I…I don't know," Noah said, regretting how the truth

sounded.

Tameron grabbed his backpack and slid it across the floor to Noah. "One way to find out."

Noah picked up the large canvas backpack and was surprised by its weight. With its bulging pockets and numerous zippers, it looked like something issued by the army. The thought of what was inside made him nervous.

"You won't fit in the rest of my gear," Tameron said, referring to his hat and jacket.

Noah nodded. As he fed his arms through the straps of the pack, Marlo flew off and landed on Tameron's shoulder. Through the backpack, Noah felt the hard curves of the tail against his spine.

Tameron used his good leg to slowly stand. "See the cords in the straps?"

Noah looked down. Near his shoulders, two cords emerged from holes circled by velvet patches.

"Pull them when you're ready."

Noah held the cords in his hands. P-Dog, seeing what Noah was doing, scurried off.

"It's gonna hurt," Tameron said.

"I know," Noah said. "Ella told me."

"But not that bad, and just for a bit."

Noah wondered what "a bit" meant to a Descender, and then gathered enough courage to pull the cords. Two *click*s sounded inside the pack, and then the weight dropped off his shoulders as the tail fell out. One end of it seemed to grab on to the base of his spine, and pricks of pain shot through his body. Light flashed across his vision and he suddenly became aware of the muscles surrounding his tailbone. He peered over his shoulder and saw the long appendage stretched across the concrete. Fifteen feet long, it was covered in armored plates and studded with a jumble of spikes. The canvas pack was gone—fused to the back of his jacket.

Noah suddenly lost his balance and dropped to one knee. His head swirled, and as more light flashed across his vision, the bronze statues seemed to glow. The magic of the Secret Zoo was inside him—he had the power of a Descender for the first time!

"Up!" Tameron said. "It'll pass; just power through it!"

Noah stood, staggered, and then found his balance. After a few seconds, the pain was gone and the dizziness stopped. He could sense the tail, all fifteen feet of it. It felt like a part of him was lying on the ground.

"Now move it," Tameron said.

Noah didn't need to ask how. He somehow knew he could move the tail just like any other part of his body. And when his thoughts went to the base of his spine, the tail curled and slid across the floor. He imagined the tail rising, and it went up and up, like a serpent from the ocean of a fantasy, brushing against an overhead rafter.

The tail. *His* tail. Noah allowed it to fall, and it thumped against the floor.

"Good," Tameron said. "Do it again—better control this time."

As he lifted the tail again, fireflies swirled along with the air. He swung the tail back and forth, and each time it reversed direction, he had to brace himself to keep from falling over.

"The column," Tameron said, pointing off to one side. "Hit it."

The steel column that Tameron was referring to was as thick as the trunk of a big oak tree. Along with dozens of other columns, it helped support the basement ceiling.

"What if it breaks?" Noah asked.

"It won't," Tameron said. "Don't worry. The ceiling isn't going anywhere."

Noah returned his thoughts to the base of his spine and whipped the tail, which glanced off the column and skipped across the floor. He stood there, surprised by the pain. "It...it hurt."

"Good," Tameron said. "I'd be worried if it didn't. Now hit it again."

Noah swung, striking the column with a solid *thump*. The spikes etched lines in the steel.

"Again," Tameron repeated.

Noah swung his tail in the opposite direction, striking

the other side of the column.

"More power this time!" Tameron said. "Put your body into it!"

Noah nodded. Then he swung his tail, which struck the column twice as hard. He winced at the way it hurt.

"Ignore the pain," Tameron said. "Or better yet, accept it."

Again, Noah swung his tail and carved more lines into the steel.

Two minutes passed. Three. As Noah continued to attack the column, the pain worsened. He hardly noticed, though. All his thoughts were on one thing: He was training as a Descender.

"Take a break," Tameron said.

Noah struck the column a final time and then allowed his tail to fall limply to the ground. His chest heaved as he fought to catch his breath. Someone clapped him on the shoulder, and he turned and saw Sam standing beside him.

"Not bad," Sam said.

Noah nodded. He tried to sit on the ground and couldn't because of his tail.

Tameron started laughing. "Good luck with that. Get out of the gear if you want to take a seat."

Noah realized that even though the straps of the backpack had fused with his jacket, the cords were still dangling near his shoulders. He pulled them and fought to keep his balance as the tail retracted into the pack. Then he winced at the pain as the tail separated from his spine. He waited a few seconds to make sure nothing else was going to happen, and then he slipped his arms out of the shoulder straps and took a seat, still struggling for breath.

"How did it feel?" Sam asked.

Noah waited a few seconds for more of his breath to return. "Good. Like…like I was lashing out."

"At what?"

He thought about it. "I don't know. Everything. And nothing. It felt…"

"Primal?" Sam said.

Noah wasn't sure what that meant, but he sensed Sam was right. "Yeah."

"It gets better," Sam said. "It gets better as *you* get better."

"We don't have time for that," Noah said. "DeGraff could attack at any moment."

"But the fight might go on for years."

Noah cringed at the thought—his world at war and Noah on the front lines.

Sam got to his feet, saying, "Let's get you back home."

Noah stood and strapped on the backpack.

"Take care of it," Tameron said. Then he winked and added, "I want it back."

Noah smiled because he didn't know what to say. Then

he followed Sam toward the portal to his closet. As he made his way, he saw Mr. Darby sitting on the bottom steps of a staircase that led to the museum above. Dozens of fireflies were flying around him—points of blinking light in the dim space. A few were resting on his velvet jacket. He was frowning and looking worried. Noah wasn't sure if he was upset about Noah coming to the Secret Zoo, DeGraff, or something else entirely. He looked strange without his usual smile. Fake.

Noah stopped and said, "Mr. Darby? You okay?"

"You're not at home," the old man said.

"I'm...I'm headed that way."

Mr. Darby's gaze shifted to the canvas bag on Noah's back. "Not a bad idea if you can manage it. Can you?"

"I...I think so." Noah realized that Mr. Darby was holding something. A photograph. "Who's in the picture?" Noah tried to see for himself, but couldn't.

Mr. Darby looked at the photo in his grasp. Seconds passed. Just when it seemed he wouldn't answer, his frown deepened, and he said, "Someone very dear to me."

Noah had no idea who he was talking about. He became curious about the stairway and all the fireflies. "What's...what's up there?"

Mr. Darby glanced over his shoulder. Then he looked back to Noah and simply said, "The truth."

Noah waited for more, but nothing came. After a few

seconds, a hand suddenly dropped on his shoulder, and he turned to see Sam.

"C'mon," the Descender said. "Let's deal with the truth another day."

Noah nodded. Then he adjusted Tameron's backpack and followed Sam across the basement.

A voice rose up from behind them: "Assuming there is another day."

As Noah continued to walk, it terrified him to know that such a desperate thought had come from the leader of the Secret Zoo.

*

Noah set Tameron's pack on the floor and then softly walked to his bedroom door. He peeked into the hall. The door to his parents' room was shut, and their lights were out—they were asleep. If they'd checked on him, the mirage had worked. He walked back across his room and put his arm on the mattress so the chameleons would know to crawl onto his body and back into his pocket. When he could no longer feel the patter of their feet, he knocked the pile of clothes to the floor and dropped into bed, his muscles already aching.

Sam sat on Noah's desk and quietly said, "You got anything to eat?"

"Drawer," Noah whispered, and it must have been obvious that he meant the desk drawer because it noisily slid open and then Noah heard the crinkle of a granola bar wrapper.

"Want one?"

Noah did, but he was too tired to chew.

Sam nodded toward Tameron's backpack. "Take it with you—everywhere you go. Especially school. It'll fit in your locker, right?"

Noah nodded, the side of his face pressed against the mattress.

"You'll need protection all the time now."

Noah imagined himself using Tameron's tail to fight off a group of sasquatches on Jenkins Street. The idea was terrifying.

A noise suddenly rose in his ear—a woman's voice: "I got something on the northeast end of...wait...never mind."

At first Noah thought he'd imagined the voice, but then he remembered his headset. On the other side of the portal, it hadn't worked to communicate with the Secret Cityzens in his neighborhood.

"Take it out," Sam said. "Get some rest."

"But you—"

"I'll be fine," Sam said. He touched his ear and added, "I'm used to this thing."

"Will you sleep?"

Sam took the last bite of the granola bar and dropped the wrapper into Noah's waste basket. "Some," he said. "The

Descenders know to stay quiet on the airwaves when people need to sleep."

"I'll never relax," Noah said.

"You don't need to relax," Sam said. "You just need to sleep."

The image of Sam began to blur, and Noah realized his eyelids were closing. The room went dark. Noah felt his heartbeat slow, and then his breathing became calm and rhythmic. Within seconds, he fell asleep.

In his dream, he battled DeGraff in the City of Species while people stood by, cheering. Noah attacked with his tail, knocking the Shadowist through brick buildings and marble fountains. And Solana stood in the crowd, cheering louder than anyone else.

CHAPTER 6

TROUBLE IN CLASS

"I can't believe this is happening!" Ella said. She pointed to the backpack Noah carried and added, "And I can't believe you're wearing that *thing* to school!"

Noah rolled his shoulders to adjust Tameron's weighty pack and said, "Sam told me to."

The scouts had met up on their walk to school. They were groggy and anxious, fearful that DeGraff might attack at any moment. All of them were wearing their Specter pants. When Clarksville Elementary came into sight, Richie said, "Why do I have a feeling this could be a very short day?"

The scouts walked up the concrete path to their school and pushed through the entrance doors. They stopped by Noah's locker first. Tameron's backpack fit, but barely. As they started to walk off, someone came up from behind them and shoved Richie against the lockers. Walt. His cronies, Dave and Doug, were with him. Steel clanged, and Richie almost fell to the floor.

"Knock it off, jerk!" Ella said. She took a step forward, but Noah jumped in between her and Walt, who'd turned

58

their way.

Walt took a few steps forward and practically pushed his chest against Noah's. "And what are you gonna do?"

"You're such an idiot," Noah said. "And what you did to my friends—that was more than just bullying. That was *assault.*"

Walt's hard stare softened and his extra-wide shoulders slumped a bit. Noah could see that Walt knew he was right. Walt had recently decked Richie and dumped out Ella's backpack, which was more than everyday schoolyard bullying.

"Break it up, boys!" someone hollered, and Noah glanced over to see Mrs. Walker standing just outside her classroom door, her hands planted on her hips.

Walt sneered at Noah, returning to his typical self. Then he swung around and headed down the hall, his shoulders swaying.

"C'mon," Ella said as she started to walk off, pulling Noah by his sleeve. "We've got enough problems right now."

The first bell rang, which meant students had three minutes to get to class. At his locker, Richie spun through his combination and opened the door. He started to hang his jacket and then suddenly jumped back.

"What's wrong?" Ella asked.

Instead of waiting for a response, Noah pulled open the

door and looked inside. A large cobweb hung in one corner, and in the middle of it was a big spider with long spiny legs and a bulbous body. Not a tarantula, but just as bad, because it was a creature from the Secret Zoo, and it looked dangerous.

Megan peered over Richie's shoulder.

"Okay," Richie said, "there are at least three hundred lockers in this school. I'm guessing this isn't the only one with a surprise inside."

"Yeah," Ella said, "looks like we didn't get all the spiders."

The nervous spider crawled as far as it could into the corner.

"What do we do?" Megan asked.

The second bell rang, and Richie jumped again.

"We go to class," Noah said. "We hope for the best, but expect the worst. And we keep an eye out for possible portals, like Mr. Darby said."

*

Megan could barely concentrate on what Mrs. Simons, her math teacher, said as she crossed out numbers on the whiteboard and arranged them in fancy ways. All her thoughts were on the Secret Zoo and what was happening in Clarksville. When she heard Jessica Hunter whisper "big spider" to someone, she leaned closer to the conversation to hear. It seemed Jessica, like Richie, had found something in her locker.

Megan impatiently tapped her toe and watched the second hand on the clock slowly sweep around. Five minutes passed. Ten. Fifteen. Every once in a while, she'd glance at Ella, who sat a few rows over in their split-grade class. Her best friend seemed just as nervous as she was.

At some point, Mrs. Simons wiped an eraser across the board and started a new math question. As Megan absently watched the numbers appear, she noticed something. The whiteboard had a metal frame that protruded about an inch from the wall, and five or six thin objects that resembled the teeth of a comb were sticking out of the gap. She focused her gaze. After a couple minutes, the objects moved a few inches in one direction, and three or four new ones appeared. Her insides dropped as she realized she was looking at the legs of an enormous insect. A creature from the Secret Zoo— something other than a spider, it seemed—was crawling in the narrow space between the whiteboard frame and the wall.

Ella was still staring blankly into space, clearly lost in her own thoughts.

"Ella," Megan said just above a whisper. "Ella!"

No response. Behind the whiteboard, the legs inched forward. Whatever was behind the metal frame wasn't going to stay a secret for long.

Megan jumped to her feet and did her best to look casual as she walked to the front of the class. Mrs. Simons paused at the distraction, then resumed teaching. Megan swiped the bathroom pass off her teacher's desk and headed for the door, shooting Ella a worried look on the way. In the hall, she found an empty bathroom. Inside, she opened a pocket on her Specter pants, and chameleons began to crawl out onto her body. She felt the patter and prick of their feet along her legs, her torso, her arms. The chameleons' colors began to swirl and blur, and within seconds, Megan was blended into the world around her.

She peeked out the bathroom door, saw no one, and slipped into the hall. Then she ran back to her class and paused outside the open door to look herself over. Perfectly camouflaged. She stepped into the room.

Mrs. Simons was calling on students, asking for input in solving an equation on the board. Ella was staring out into the hall, clearly worried about Megan. Ella couldn't see her—and that meant no one could.

Megan silently walked to the front of the class. More of the legs of the insect, whatever it was, were showing now. It didn't look like the other students in the room had noticed.

She slowly walked to the board. Seconds later, she was behind the long desk at the front of the class, her teacher only a few steps away. If she could get a small chameleon to latch onto the insect, the chameleon would know to camouflage it. Then Megan could grab both creatures and take them out of the room.

"Who else has an idea?" Mrs. Simons asked, and it seemed like she was responding to Megan's thoughts.

In the back of the room, Peter Ryan raised his hand.

"Yes, Peter," Mrs. Simons said. As she turned and took a step toward Peter, Megan slipped in behind her. She grabbed a tiny chameleon off her shoulder, reached for the top of the whiteboard, and panicked when her hand stopped a few inches short. She stood on the tips of her toes and stretched as far as she could. It wasn't enough.

"That's possible, Peter," Mrs. Simons said. "Can you explain yourself a bit?"

Her teacher had taken another step away from her desk. The students who weren't staring off into space were scribbling on their papers, either doodling or taking notes. Megan noticed Mrs. Simons's padded chair, which sat on five rollers. If she could get it closer to the wall, she might be able to stand on it and reach the top of the whiteboard.

She grabbed the chair and slowly rolled it back a few inches. She paused and watched the class—no one had noticed. She rolled it back a few more inches, and then a few more. Mrs. Simons had walked over to Peter, who was now pointing out something in his textbook. Megan stopped rolling the chair when the back of it touched the wall.

Go! a voice inside her said.

She carefully stood on the chair and faced the whiteboard. She could now see most of the creature. It had dozens of orange legs and a brown segmented body. It wasn't an insect—it was an arthropod, a giant centipede, and the scouts had had encounters with them before. Wondering how it had gotten behind the whiteboard, Megan looked around until she saw a wide crack in a ceiling tile. At some point before class, the centipede must have fallen through and landed on the whiteboard, and now it couldn't get down.

"That's close, Peter," Mrs. Simons said. "But let me show you something."

Mrs. Simons was walking to the front of the room.

Megan reached out and dropped the chameleon on the centipede, which quickly began to disappear. The centipede, still barely visible, squirmed and fell off the whiteboard, the chameleon clinging to its back. Megan instinctively reached for the creatures, but she lost her balance and the chair rolled out from beneath her, crashing into the teacher's desk.

Mrs. Simons stopped in mid-sentence, and the room fell silent. Megan lay on the floor, her side aching and her heart racing. To her left was the wall with the whiteboard, and to her right were the desks of the first row of students. She glanced up and saw the worried expressions of Quinn Neubert, Tina Garner, and Stella Diehl. The sixth graders were staring at Mrs. Simons's chair as if it had just rolled off a spaceship.

Megan noticed a ghostly shape in front of the wall. The chameleon had fallen off the centipede, which was now slowly coming out of its camouflage.

"Who did that?" Mrs. Simons said, and Megan realized she was talking about her chair.

Before the centipede could come into full view, the chameleon pounced on it, blending it back into its surroundings.

Quinn stared in Megan's direction, his eyes wide and his jaw hanging open. He glanced at Tina and Stella and said, "Did you see that?" But the girls were focused on Mrs. Simons, who was still trying to figure out who had kicked her chair.

Megan got up as quietly as she could and grabbed the centipede by pinching a spot behind its head. Then she quickly walked out of the room and stood in the hall, unsure what to do. Could she hide the centipede somewhere? Her locker? If only she could get to a portal to the Secret Zoo.

An idea struck her. A portal. She remembered how the scouts had used their Specter pants to drain the water out of the barricaded hallway in the Secret Creepy Critters. Her pockets connected to the Secret Zoo!

The hall was empty. She opened the big zipper on the right leg of her pants, and as the chameleons raced into her pocket, she dropped the centipede—and the chameleon on its back—in with them. Within seconds, the patter and pull of little feet stopped, and Megan's camouflage was gone.

Still, no one was around. She touched the transmit

button on her tiny earpiece and softly said, "Evie?"

After a few seconds, Evie's voice rose in her ear: "Yeah?"

"I need you at the school. Bring the Specters—all of them."

A pause, and then Evie's voice again: "We're on our way. Full camo?"

"Yeah," Megan said. "And be ready to use your pockets to send some animals to the Secret Zoo."

"You got it," Evie said, and then the radio waves went silent.

Megan adjusted her clothes—a pull here, a tug there. Then she fluffed up her pigtails, took out her hall pass, and walked back into the classroom.

Mrs. Simons was standing in front of the whiteboard, scowling at the group. A few students near her desk were nervously accusing one another. In the front row, Quinn was leaning toward Stella, saying something and pointing to the floor. Megan strolled up to the scene, pretending to be confused by the commotion. Then she set the hall pass on Mrs. Simons's desk and said, "Did I miss something?" to anyone who might be listening.

As she walked to her seat, she noticed Ella, who'd raised an eyebrow at her in a curious way.

CHAPTER 7

NOT-SO-WIDE WALT

When school was dismissed, Noah went to his locker and pressed his forehead against the flimsy metal. He was exhausted. The Specters, knowing it was critical to keep the dangerous animals away from the students and to continue to keep the Secret Zoo a secret, had spent hours covertly combing the school to get rid of centipedes, tarantulas, and other insects from closets, the playground, and back rooms. They'd even cracked the combinations on the lockers to round up any Secret Zoo creatures inside.

The scouts didn't know how the Secret Zoo creatures had gotten into their school. A hidden portal, perhaps, like Mr. Darby had said. And they didn't know if the creatures were part of DeGraff's plan—a diversion to keep the scouts and Specters busy. Or were they just an unintended effect of DeGraff's new portals?

As Noah dialed in his combination, he jumped at a loud voice in his ear: "HEY!"

He glanced over his shoulder and came face-to-face with Wide Walt. The school bully was smiling, his plump cheeks looking as red and round as tomatoes. Dave and

Doug, Walt's friends, were standing off to the side, snickering in their usual way.

Noah shook his head and finished dialing his combination. "Get out of here, Walt," he said as he swung open his locker door. He put his math book on his shelf, adding, "I'm in no mood."

"What's in the bag, bro?"

Noah realized Walt was talking about Tameron's backpack. When the bully suddenly reached into the locker, Noah swatted his hand away.

"Don't," Noah said.

"*C'mon*—what's in it? Something else that's gonna bite me?"

Walt had recently stuck his hand in Ella's backpack when P-Dog was hiding in it. He'd spent the next few days with a row of pinpricks on his fat finger.

No parents were around, and the teachers were still in their classes.

Walt laughed and reached into Noah's locker again. This time Noah turned and pushed Walt in the chest, hard. The school bully lost his balance and stumbled backward a few steps. He stood and stared at his chest, his mouth hanging open. Dave and Doug had stopped smiling.

He raised his gaze to Noah's face. "You serious, bro?"

The locker clanged as Noah quickly threw his notebook on the shelf. "Just...don't, Walt. Okay?"

The way Walt casually glanced over his shoulders made Noah nervous. He turned and squared his body to Walt. He wasn't going to back down, not today. When someone grabbed his arm, he looked and saw Ella. Richie and Megan were standing behind her.

"Don't do this," Ella said. "Let's just go home."

Something about the idea made him feel sick. Just leave, just run, just cower—just let Walt continue to have his way with the students at Clarksville Elementary. He eyed Ella and then softly shook his head. He wanted to say something, but the storm of emotions he was feeling was making it difficult to think.

"C'mon, let's—"

He rolled his shoulder to get away from Ella. Then he took a step toward Walt.

The noises in the hall had blended into a single sound. Noah barely noticed as students continued to rush by, bumping into one another while making for the exits.

Stop him, a voice inside him said, and Noah realized it wasn't his own, not really. It was Sam's.

Noah took another step.

"Dude's gone cray-cray!" Walt said to his friends. He'd wanted to sound funny and brave, but Noah had heard the nervous waver in his voice. Walt took a step forward. They stared into each other's eyes like boxers before the first bell.

"Noah—*stop!*" Megan said.

He thought of Sam, Tameron, and the other Descenders. He thought of DeGraff, Charlie Red, and what might happen to his world at any moment. And before he knew what he was doing, his punch had been thrown. The school bully fell backward and his head thumped against the ground. Walt rolled from side to side, grimacing in pain. He made no attempt to get up.

"*Stop it!*" Megan called out.

Noah realized the halls had gone silent. All the students were watching, glancing between Noah and the boy who had bullied them for years.

Richie appeared at Noah's side, saying, "Let's go, Noah!"

Noah stared down at Walt, his entire body trembling. A part of him wanted to help Walt up, but another part of him wanted to deliver a second blow. He felt nervous, proud, and ashamed. After a few seconds, he turned to his locker and quickly put on his jacket. Then he grabbed his backpack and slipped his arms through the straps. The weight of the pack felt good, familiar. He felt strong with it on.

Megan ran up the hall, followed by Ella and Richie. Noah took a step and stared at Dave and Doug, who were standing by in shock.

Try something, Noah thought. *Do something—make a move.* But Dave and Doug backed up instead.

"Noah—*c'mon!*"

Richie was waving for Noah to follow him. Noah saw Walt still lying on the floor. He was hurt, and a part of Noah felt sick because he was to blame. But then Noah remembered all the times Walt had hurt his friends. Walt had never cared—not once.

But that's Walt, a voice inside him said, and this time it was his own. *Not you. You care.*

He considered this. Then he raised his leg high, stepped over Walt, and headed for the exit, the backpack shifting on his shoulders with each stride.

CHAPTER 8

THE MULTIPOINT

"Good afternoon, Noah."

Noah jumped, stumbled backward through the doorway, and fell onto his front porch. From his sudden seat on the cold concrete, he stared at the person on his living room couch—an old man with long gray hair pulled back in a ponytail, a bushy beard, and a pair of dark sunglasses.

"Mr. Darby…"

The old man forced a smile.

Noah continued to sit on the porch, the cold seeping into his legs, the weighty backpack pulling down on his shoulders.

"Are you coming in?" Mr. Darby asked.

Noah nodded, but didn't get up.

"Soon?"

Noah stood, walked into his house, and stopped just inside the doorway. He tried to say something, but the words were a jumble of letters in his brain.

"You might want to shut the door," Mr. Darby said as he pulled the long flaps of his velvet jacket closed. "It's a bit drafty."

Noah did and then slowly regained most of his senses. "What's…what's going on?"

"Oh…I'm just sitting on your couch." He gazed around the room—the bookshelf, the television, the pictures on the wall. "And remembering."

"Remembering what?"

"Better times, I suppose."

Noah had no idea what Mr. Darby was talking about. He walked deeper into the room and tossed Tameron's backpack on a chair.

"Careful with that," Mr. Darby said. "It's not full of textbooks, you know."

Noah glanced into the kitchen, then up the staircase leading to the second floor.

"Your parents are still at work," Mr. Darby said. "Otherwise I wouldn't be so casual. Where's Megan?"

"Ella's house, with Evie." Noah looked around. "Where's Sam?"

"Back at the Institute of Light, checking on things. And Blizzard's in the shed, doing fine. Sam fed him some things from your fridge. You should ghost him later and let him walk around in your backyard for a bit. Just make sure your parents aren't watching. Polar bears tend to leave big footprints."

Noah nodded. With everything that was going on, he'd practically forgotten about Blizzard.

Mr. Darby casually picked at a few pieces of lint caught in the folds of his jacket and added, "Please pardon the intrusion. I invited myself again. The portal in your closet...most convenient. Tell me about what happened at your school today."

Noah took a seat on the couch and told him everything—the spiders, the centipedes, the Specters. Mr. Darby combed his fingers through his beard and seemed to contemplate things. When Noah was finished, he stared at Mr. Darby's dark sunglasses and wondered about the old man's eyes—his milky eyes, which he'd accidentally revealed to the scouts outside the Secret Creepy Critters a few days earlier.

"DeGraff is staging his army," Mr. Darby said. "That's the only explanation." The old man stood and slowly paced across the floor. "He's building portals to new places, preparing to attack, like we feared. There's a portal in your school, Noah, and the Secret Zoo creatures are coming through it."

"On purpose?"

"Perhaps. In any regard, this makes what I'm here to show you more critical than ever." He reached into his jacket pocket and pulled out four pieces of velvet, each the size of a washcloth. He held the pieces by their corners, and Noah understood why—they were full of the magic that could portal objects to new places. "The Multipoint Portal," he said as he walked over to Noah. "It's a project that our Teknikals and magical scientists have been working on. You've been to Kangaroo Kampground, yes?"

Noah nodded and remembered the times he'd crossed that sector, portaling from one small tent to another.

"Their development lab. Council has had an interest in the Multipoint for years."

The old man looked around the room until his gaze settled on a shelf that held a bunch of dusty knickknacks. Then he reached out to Noah, grasping a piece of velvet by its corner. "I'd like you to hold this above your lap. It's best to keep your fingers away from the center."

Noah used both hands to carefully hold the velvet cloth about ten inches over his legs.

Mr. Darby walked to the shelf with the knickknacks. He lifted a velvet cloth a few inches above an old fisherman with a yellow hat and turned to Noah, saying, "Ready?"

Unsure what Mr. Darby was doing, Noah nodded.

Mr. Darby dropped the velvet on top of the knickknack, which disappeared and immediately fell from the piece of cloth in Noah's hands, landing in his lap. A portal. Nothing spectacular—Noah had seen this before.

Mr. Darby released a second piece of velvet over another knickknack, a woman playing the piano, and the knickknack immediately fell onto Noah's lap next to the fisherman. This was a new trick: two portals that joined to the same spot.

Noah looked up in time to see Mr. Darby drop the last piece of velvet over a clown with an oversized nose. The knickknack fell onto Noah's lap with a *clink!* of porcelain.

"The Multipoint Portal," Mr. Darby said again. "Several gateways joined to a single spot."

Surprised, Noah looked at the porcelain figurines and considered this. The clown was upside down, his white head planted between Noah's knees.

Mr. Darby carefully gathered the pieces of velvet from the shelf. Then he walked over to Noah, took away his velvet, and neatly folded all the pieces before gently placing them in his pocket.

"A new magic," Mr. Darby said. "And an emergency strategy."

Noah had no idea what the old man was getting at.

"Think of the portals in the Clarksville Zoo," Mr. Darby said. "What if we could make them open to a single spot—a secure spot within the Secret Zoo? What if we could contain DeGraff's army, stop it from invading your world?"

Noah sat up so straight that one of the knickknacks, the woman playing the piano, fell to the carpet. "How?"

"How *what*, Noah?"

"The curtains at the Clarksville Zoo—they're designed to open to different spots."

"They just need to be *re*designed," Mr. Darby said. He

tapped his pocket and added, "Like these."

"Can you do that?"

"Yes. But can we do it in time? That I don't know." Mr. Darby stroked his beard to a point and added, "The portal will need to lead to a big, open space. We have a place in mind: the courtyard in Koala Kastle."

Noah considered everything. "So any animal on its way to the Clarksville Zoo would end up in Koala Kastle instead?"

"Correct." The old man became quiet for a bit and then added, "There is one issue, though."

Noah waited for Mr. Darby to continue. The seconds that passed seemed like eternity.

"We can't reverse the magic," Mr. Darby said at last.

"What…what do you mean?"

"Once we implement the Multipoint, we can't change the portals back."

"So you're saying that every portal in the Clarksville Zoo will have a one-way ticket to Koala Kastle? Forever?"

"Correct. The portals will never function correctly again. They'll be decommissioned. Our worlds will become separate."

Noah slowly shook his head. The Secret Zoo, gone forever. Podgy, Blizzard, Little Bighorn—he would never see them again.

"I'm afraid the time has come for Operation Division,"

Mr. Darby said. "An emergency plan for the segregation of the Secret Zoo from your world. It's been known for years, and reserved for a moment such as this." Mr. Darby frowned, and his shoulders slumped. He slowly shook his head, and it was clear to Noah that he hated the idea of the zoos dividing.

"But the animals...your mission. The Secret Society protects endangered—"

"The work of the Secret Society wouldn't end," Mr. Darby said. "Its individual groups would continue to protect endangered species, just in secret pockets around the world, like they once did."

Noah didn't understand at first, but then he remembered that some Crossers lived on the Outside. Policemen, teachers, politicians—all were part of the Secret Society, a band of humans committed to animal conservation. He opened his mouth to protest but words wouldn't come. He thought of his animal friends again. Podgy, Blizzard, Marlo—gone forever.

"There has to be another way," Noah said. He stood up and the two knickknacks still in his lap dropped to the carpet. "There must—"

"There *isn't*," Mr. Darby said. "And right now, we need to focus on keeping our worlds safe, and what is necessary to do that."

Noah reluctantly nodded and tried not to think about

saying good-bye to his animal friends for the last time.

Mr. Darby picked up the fallen knickknacks. As he returned them to the shelf, Noah glanced out the window toward the street and thought about everything. Just outside his door, a war was brewing.

"Mr. Darby?"

"Yes?"

"Are you scared?"

The old man smiled, but there was no joy in it. "I've been scared for a long time, young man."

"About the Secret Zoo?"

"About...lots of things."

Mr. Darby was acting strangely, just like he had the previous day in the Institute of Light. As Noah watched the leader of the Secret Society organize the knickknacks, he said, "Can I ask you something?"

"Of course."

"The other day, on the staircase in the museum, you were holding something. A photograph."

Mr. Darby continued to arrange the knickknacks. "Yes."

"Who was in the picture?"

Mr. Darby clasped his hands behind his back. Then he slowly turned and faced Noah. "I think it would be best to stay focused on our current predicament. The past isn't something we can—"

"No!" Noah said, surprised by his sharp tone. "I need to know what's going on—with you."

Mr. Darby raised his eyebrows above his sunglasses. "With *me*?"

"Yeah," Noah said. "With you."

"Sorry, Noah—I don't understand."

"You have a jacket that's made from the same velvet used for the portals—a jacket that keeps you from getting sick."

"Sick? What are you—"

"The time at Chickadee Lane—you came to the Clarksville Zoo without your jacket and stayed too long. You couldn't keep your balance, and you started forgetting things. You even forgot the names of the animals, which you *never* do."

"I...I don't recall."

But it was clear by his hesitation that he did recall.

"And there are other weird things, too. Like the time the Descenders let DeGraff escape. You got mad at them, and they kneeled in front of you, right in the street. They bowed to you like you were a king." Noah recalled the sight of the Descenders, each on one knee. "Are you, Mr. Darby? Are you a king?"

Mr. Darby almost laughed. "I'm no king, dear boy." He looked away and added, "I'm a man, just like any other."

Noah took a slow step toward Mr. Darby, saying, "But

you have a secret. And I think it's even bigger than the Secret Zoo."

Mr. Darby adjusted his sunglasses and kept quiet.

"What is it? What's your secret?"

The old man's gaze went to the window, the foyer, the blank television screen—anything but Noah.

"*C'mon,*" Noah said. "Think of all that's happened between us. Don't you trust me yet?"

"Trust is not the issue," Mr. Darby shot back.

"Then what is?"

Mr. Darby seemed to think about something for a minute. "The unwillingness to go to a place I'd rather forget."

Noah had no idea what the old man was talking about.

After a few seconds, Mr. Darby added, "Do you recall the story of Frederick and his father, Mr. Jackson?"

Noah tried to remember. Frederick was the young son of Mr. Jackson, a rich businessman in Clarksville who created the Clarksville Zoo after the tragic death of his wife. "Yeah," Noah said. "Most of it."

"Do you remember Simon the Simian?"

Noah nodded. "Mr. Jackson and Frederick were out for a walk one day and they came across a barn. The farmer was moving, and he had a strange pet that he couldn't take with him. A monkey."

"A langur," Mr. Darby said in a lifeless tone. "Simon

made Frederick smile for the first time in years, and Mr. Jackson took the monkey home, no questions asked. Mr. Jackson built a cage for Simon in his yard, and people came from all around to see him." Mr. Darby began to stroll across the room, saying, "Soon, people began to show up with other unwanted animals—exotic creatures, most of them. The animals made Frederick so happy that Mr. Jackson couldn't turn them away. He built more and more cages on his property, and the Clarksville Zoo was born."

Hearing the story again reminded Noah of the first time he'd heard it, the day the scouts had discovered the Secret Zoo. In Hummingbird Hideout, they'd listened to Mr. Darby tell the tale while hummingbirds darted around them, streaks of color across a green landscape. It had been so long ago, but in a way, it felt like yesterday.

Mr. Darby turned and looked at a wall covered with family photographs, his back to Noah. As he began to scan the pictures, he said, "I'm sure you remember the part that comes next."

"Frederick died," Noah said. "In his sleep, just before he turned thirteen."

Mr. Darby nodded. "And the best part of Mr. Jackson died with him, I'm afraid." His attention stopped on a picture of Noah playing football with his father. "How old are you in this one?" he asked in his strange flat tone.

"About nine," Noah said, his tone equally flat as he

tried to figure things out. "Maybe ten."

"Frederick's age," Mr. Darby said, "when his mother died." He leaned in for a closer look at the picture and said, "Frederick never knew such happiness at that age. Can you imagine losing your mother the way he did?"

Noah quickly shook his head. He remembered how he'd felt when Megan was missing. He'd had an endless ache—not just in his body, but in his soul.

Mr. Darby slowly walked over to another picture, one of Megan standing in her swimsuit by a blue lake. A young teenage boy was standing beside her. "Who's this?"

"My cousin. From Florida."

Mr. Darby nodded. He reached up and touched the picture. "Frederick was this age when he died."

"How did it happen?" Noah asked. "I mean, I know he died in his sleep, but how?"

"The doctors never figured it out," Mr. Darby said as he held his gaze on the boy who reminded him of Frederick. "They had…suspicions."

"Suspicions? What…what do you mean?"

Instead of answering, Mr. Darby took a closer look at another picture, saying, "All these memories—all these life experiences. You are blessed, Noah."

"I know," Noah said, but without much conviction. Mr. Darby was beginning to make him nervous.

Mr. Darby took a step and focused on another picture,

one of Megan and Noah playing in the snow. "Frederick was buried on a cold gray day, much like"—he tapped his fingertip on the frame—"this. The day had been a blur for Mr. Jackson, and he had been too stunned for tears. But he wept upon returning to his empty house—he wept for days."

Noah wondered how Mr. Darby could possibly know this. As far as Noah knew, Mr. Darby and Mr. Jackson had never been friends.

"Mr. Jackson spent hours roaming from room to room in his cold, empty house, almost as if he expected to find something. Frederick. Or Frederick's mother, perhaps. He was suddenly so alone. Most nights, he'd sit on Frederick's empty bed and pretend to be with his boy."

There was no way Mr. Darby could know these things. Was he making them up?

Mr. Darby walked to another place along the wall. Noah kept quiet, suddenly lacking courage to speak.

"A good life, Noah," Mr. Darby said as he looked at a picture of Noah's mother holding Noah as a baby.

Noah tried to say *I know*, but the words wouldn't come.

"Mr. Jackson sank into depression, and then madness. His dreams, when he managed to sleep, were filled with bleak memories."

Noah couldn't stand it any longer. "How can you *possibly* know all this?"

Mr. Darby stood up straight and clasped his hands

behind his back. Then he slowly turned and faced Noah. His expression was so dull that Noah could barely see any resemblance to the kind man he knew.

"Noah," the old man said, "*I* am Mr. Jackson."

Noah's insides dropped. He took a step back, still staring at Mr. Darby, and bumped into an end table. The room seemed to teeter one way and then another.

"What...what are you talking about?"

"I'm Frederick's father."

Noah shook his head. "Mr. Jackson's *dead*!"

"Perhaps," the old man conceded. "But Mr. Darby is very much alive."

Noah continued to shake his head. The old man liked to talk in riddles—was he doing that now?

"It's the magic," Noah said as he took a slow step away from Mr. Darby. "In your jacket. The magic is keeping you alive, just like the magic in DeGraff's coat is keeping *him* alive."

Mr. Darby reached toward Noah, saying, "Trust that I—"

A low rumble invaded the room. Noah and Mr. Darby looked out the window and saw a vehicle pulling up the driveway. Noah's mother was home.

Noah grabbed Mr. Darby by the sleeve of his jacket. "C'mon—you have to go!"

Mr. Darby nodded, and the two of them quickly headed

upstairs to Noah's bedroom. Noah ran to his window and peered out. His mother was taking something from her trunk—a bag of groceries. Noah turned around, expecting to see Mr. Darby making his way to the portal in his closet. Instead, the old man was looking around the room.

"Mr. Darby! You have to get out of here!"

"His room was like yours, Noah," Mr. Darby said. "Trinkets and games—boys haven't changed so much in a hundred years."

"*Mr. Darby!*" Noah shouted. The old man looked his way, and Noah pointed to the closet.

"Yes," Mr. Darby said. He headed across the room, adding, "You're right."

Noah followed him into the closet. At the portal, Mr. Darby paused and looked back. "What if we can't stop him, Noah?"

"Huh?"

"DeGraff is powerful—surely you've seen that."

It pained Noah to hear the old man sounding so weak, so unexpectedly. "We will. The Multipoint—we'll make it work." Noah thought of his family and his good life—all the pictures that Mr. Darby had pointed out on the wall. He had to keep his family safe from DeGraff, no matter what.

"And if we can't?"

Noah thought of the backpack by his front door—the incredible power inside it. "Then we'll fight. Win or lose, we'll fight the same."

"Yes," Mr. Darby said. "A fight will feel good." The old man's expression changed. "Noah...there's more to the story."

"More?"

Mr. Darby nodded.

Noah heard the front door open. "Tell me later. You have to go."

"Don't forget to take care of Blizzard," Mr. Darby said. Then he stepped through the curtain and fled Noah's world.

CHAPTER 9

UNSEALING THE CEILING

"This way!" Ella said. "Are you even behind me?"

"Yeah, right here," Evie said.

The two girls were making their way through the halls of Clarksville Elementary just after eight o'clock at night. They were in full camouflage. Getting into Clarksville Elementary had been easy enough; it wasn't difficult to sneak into places when you had a magical key and could walk around like a ghost. And getting out of Ella's house hadn't been an issue because it was her mother's bowling league night. The other scouts and Specters had stayed back, mostly because getting the scouts out of their houses would have been difficult.

"Here," Ella said as she pointed to the ROOM 112 sign beside the door to her classroom, before realizing Evie couldn't see her. She checked the handle—locked. Ella fit the key into the lock and then pushed open the door. Inside the room, there was no risk of being seen, and the girls came out of their camouflage. Ella turned on the lights.

"Over there," Ella said as she pointed to the front of the

room. The girls weaved between the student desks and stepped in behind Mrs. Simons's. "See the hole?" She pointed to the tile just above the whiteboard. "Megan thinks the centipede fell through that."

Evie tucked her long bangs behind her ear and glanced around the room. Then she walked over to one side of Mrs. Simons's desk and said, "C'mon—help me."

Ella, knowing what Evie had in mind, moved to the opposite side of the desk, and the girls carried it over to the wall with the whiteboard. Evie heaved a chair onto the desktop, scattering a stack of papers and knocking over a picture of a buck-toothed girl with braces: Mrs. Simons's daughter.

Ella jumped onto the desk and said, "I'll check it out—you hold the chair." Then she stood on the plastic seat, squatting a bit so her head wouldn't touch the ceiling. She planted her hands on the tile with the piece missing. Then she applied a little pressure, and the square tile shifted in its metal frame—it was going to be easy to move.

"Ready?" Ella asked.

"Ready," Evie answered, still clutching the legs of the chair.

Ella pushed softly. The tile slowly rose—one inch, two.

The space above the ceiling revealed as a thin black gap. Ella peered into it. "I can't see anything," she said. "It's too—"

A creature fell through the gap and dangled near her head. It had dozens of pointy legs and a long segmented body—another giant centipede. It whipped back and forth, and when its hard head touched Ella's wrist, Ella freaked and dropped one arm. The ceiling tile tipped and more than a dozen centipedes came pouring out. They rained down on Evie, a few landing on her shoulders and back, one getting caught in her hair.

Ella fell off the chair. She came down hard on the desk and then rolled onto the floor. When she felt dozens of little pricks on her neck, she grabbed the end of a long centipede and flung it across the room. Then she jumped up. The centipedes were crawling around the legs of the desks, fleeing to new places. One was trying to burrow beneath a mat.

Squirming and groaning, Evie swatted two centipedes off her body. Then she gestured toward the ceiling. "Are there more?"

"I didn't see."

Evie hopped onto Mrs. Simons's desk, saying, "I need a light—a flashlight or something."

Ella knew emergency items were kept in the back of the room. She retrieved the flashlight and gave it to Evie.

Evie, standing on the chair, aimed the beam of the light into the dark opening and slowly stood up straight. Her head went into the ceiling, and then her neck and shoulders. She swept the flashlight beam around, and in its dim glow, Ella could see the Specter's worried face. Then she jumped to the top of the desk, and then to the floor.

"What's up there?" Ella asked.

Evie simply stood with her arms at her sides, the flashlight making a bright circle on the floor. She looked off into a distant part of the room.

"Evie—what's wrong?"

No answer. The Specter continued to stare into space.

Ella snatched the flashlight from Evie and climbed onto the table. She started to step onto the chair, but stopped. A part of her didn't want to see what Evie had—a part of her was too afraid. But she got up anyway, stood up straight, and aimed the beam of the flashlight into the darkness. She flinched and almost fell. The hidden space above the ceiling was infested with giant centipedes. As many as a hundred were crawling over the tops of the tiles and one another, their smooth bodies gleaming in the beam of the flashlight.

Ella jumped down to the floor and said, "There's a portal—somewhere close."

Evie glanced around. "Where?"

There were two closets in her classroom, and Ella checked them both. Nothing. She looked up at the ceiling, listened closely, and could faintly hear the patter of tiny feet. She followed the noise across the room and then put her ear against a wall. The noises were twice as loud. She jumped back and looked at Evie.

"What?" Evie said. "What is it?"

"The portal…it's in the wall."

Evie's expression froze. She ran past Ella, pressed her ear to the wall for a few seconds, and then pulled her head away.

"Mr. Darby's right," Ella said. "DeGraff's opening new portals."

Neither spoke for what seemed a long time. Then Evie touched the transmit button on her headset and said, "Girls— what's your location?"

One of the Specters, Jordynn, said, "We're scattered along the perimeter of the Clarksville Zoo, keeping an eye on things. What do you need?"

"Help," Evie said. "At Clarksville Elementary again. And as soon as possible."

CHAPTER 10

BACK TO THE BASEMENT

"They're in bed," Noah whispered as he softly closed his bedroom door.

Sam, standing by the closet, nodded.

Noah glanced at his clock. It was just after nine o'clock. His parents had retired to their bedroom, where they would likely watch television and read for the next hour before falling asleep. Megan was in her room as well. The scouts—and all the Secret Cityzens tuned to their radio frequency—had just learned what Evie and Ella had discovered at Clarksville Elementary. Everyone had decided to let Ella and the Specters handle it.

Noah went to his bed, stuffed a wad of dirty clothes beneath his covers, and opened a pocket on his Specter pants, alerting chameleons to crawl out. He concentrated his thoughts, and a minute later, his mirage was complete. Noah, seeing what appeared to be himself lying in bed, took a step back, his gaze fixed on the illusion.

"It's just...creepy," he said.

Sam pointed to Tameron's backpack, which was lying on the floor. "C'mon—let's go."

Noah slipped his arms through the shoulder straps. Then he touched the transmit button on his earpiece and said, "Guys?"

"What's up?" Richie answered.

"Sam and I are going to the museum to practice with Tameron's gear. I'll be back—an hour at the most."

"What about Mom and Dad?" Megan asked. "You better create a mirage again."

"I already did," Noah said. "Megan—you know how to find me if you need to."

"Yep," Megan said. "You're just around the corner."

The scouts wished Noah good luck, and then he and Sam walked into his closet and through the portal to the Institute of Light.

The Descenders, some sitting around and others standing guard, turned their attention to Sam, expectantly. Sam told them about the centipedes in Clarksville Elementary and the hidden portal in the wall. When he finished updating everyone, he said, "Noah's going to train for a bit." Then he turned to Noah and said, "Gear up."

Noah pulled the cords on his shoulder straps and braced himself for the pain. The tail dropped to the ground. He glanced over his shoulder. The tail was stretched out— fifteen feet of destruction, if he could use it right.

"Let's start with the column again," Sam said.

As Noah prepared to go to work, the prairie dogs

cleared the floor. It was easy to swing the tail the way he wanted, but more difficult to get power behind the movements. He concentrated on the temporary muscles near the base of his spine.

"Okay," Sam said after a few minutes. "Let's try something new. Curl the end of your tail."

Noah concentrated on the last few feet of his tail, which was lying on the ground beside him. After a few seconds, he was able to curl it inward. Then he was able to bend it the other way.

"Good," Sam said. He pointed to a life-sized statue of a polar bear standing on its hind legs, something that had probably once been in the museum. "Now grab that statue."

"Grab it?"

Sam nodded. "With your tail."

Noah thought about it. After a few seconds, he swept his tail along the floor. He was able to squeeze the statue and drag it to a new spot.

"Now throw it," Sam said, pointing to an empty area in the basement. "There."

When Noah tried, his tail slipped off the statue and slid along the ground.

"Try again," Sam said.

Noah tried, but couldn't pick the statue up.

"Again," Sam instructed. "Don't hesitate—hesitation creates doubt, and doubt leads to failure."

When Noah tried a third time, the statue wobbled, but that was it. Sam didn't say *Again*, but his stare communicated the command. Noah glanced around. Everyone was watching, even the prairie dogs. He grabbed the statue again and again, but he wasn't able to throw it. Sweat beaded on his brow, and he realized how hard he was working. Sam stood nearby, his arms crossed.

Noah angrily pulled the cords on his shoulder straps, and the tail retracted. He let the pack fall to the ground, took a seat on a nearby box, and tried to catch his breath. After a few seconds, he said, "I can't do it."

"That's crap," Sam said. "I've seen enough from you to know that you can. Now get up and try again."

"I can't *breathe*."

"You're breathing," Sam said. "Now get up."

"No," Noah said, suddenly angry at Sam's persistence and frustrated with himself. "I'm done. We can try again later."

Sam took a quick step toward Noah and the zippers on his jacket jingled. "There is no later. DeGraff isn't waiting."

"I'm not asking DeGraff to wait," Noah said. "I'm telling you to."

All across the basement, nervous whispering started.

"Get up," Sam said, and he took another step toward Noah. "You've got three seconds."

"I'm not—"

But before Noah could finish, two hands pushed against his chest and he fell off the box to the ground. He stared up at Sam, who now seemed to tower above him. As he tried to stand, Sam pushed him down again. Then the Descender picked up Tameron's backpack and threw it onto Noah's stomach.

"Put it back on," Sam said. He turned, walked to a clearing, and faced Noah again. "Grab the statue and hit me. I'm your target."

The whispers became nervous chatter.

Noah could barely believe what he'd heard. He shook his head.

"Hit me," Sam said. "Remember—you're on the ground because I put you there. Aren't you embarrassed?"

Noah shook his head. But in truth, he was. Backing down from Sam felt like backing down from Wide Walt.

"You should be," Sam said. "As a matter of fact, you—"

Noah jumped to his feet and, at the same time, slipped on the backpack. He pulled the cords in the shoulder straps and the tail connected. Then he concentrated his thoughts on the base of his spine. His tail swung, and the last few feet of it curled around the statue. The polar bear flew through the air at Sam, who quickly pulled two zippers on his jacket, releasing his wings. The Descender flew straight up, almost hitting the tall ceiling, and the statue passed beneath him and crashed harmlessly into a stack of boxes.

Sam landed and allowed his silver wings to fall to his sides. He looked at Noah and smiled. "Use your anger to focus," he said. "That's what Descenders do."

Noah didn't know what to say. He'd been baited into reacting—that much was obvious. But he'd succeeded in throwing the statue, and right now, that felt good.

"Nice work," Sam said.

Noah swelled with pride. And for the first time, he felt like he belonged to something other than the scouts, a friendship rooted in a childhood that was quickly slipping away.

*

Noah wiped the sweat off his forehead and thought about the time, guessing it was just after ten o'clock. He looked around the basement and noticed the stairway to the floor above. Fireflies dotted the dim space with points of bright light.

"Is he up there?" Noah asked.

Sam followed Noah's gaze. "Darby? Yeah, big man's probably upstairs, checking on things."

"Things?"

"The City of Species. I heard he spent most of last night staring out a window at what's left of his city."

His city. These words had never been more true. Mr. Darby was Mr. Jackson, the man who'd helped build the

Secret Zoo.

Sam motioned to the staircase. "Go. We have a few minutes. I want to talk to Tameron anyway."

Noah looked at the stairs and wondered what was up there. The truth, Mr. Darby had said. And Noah wanted to hear the rest of the old man's story.

"Go on," Sam said.

Noah nodded. As he headed across the basement, Marlo touched down on his shoulder. Noah took the steps two at a time, and at the top one, he was met with a peculiar light—constant, but alternating between dim and bright. The halls of the museum were speckled with the light of a thousand fireflies. It looked like a magical starry sky had been captured in the space around him.

"Mr. Darby?" Noah half whispered.

"Over here," came a voice, and Noah saw Mr. Darby standing by a large window, his hands clasped behind his back and the end of his flowing jacket dangling by his heels.

Noah took a slow step toward the old man, suddenly feeling like he was intruding.

"Come," Mr. Darby said. "Let me show you something."

Marlo chirped in encouragement.

As Noah headed toward the window, he gazed at the rows of gaudy gold frames on the walls. Paintings and photographs showed different animals in various habitats.

Fireflies flew all around, their light reflecting in the glass and glossy paint. As Noah approached Mr. Darby, he suddenly stopped, barely able to believe what he was seeing outside the window.

"Don't be afraid," Mr. Darby said as he continued to look outside. "The time for that is over."

Noah took a step. Then another. His feet felt like huge weights, more difficult to maneuver than Tameron's tail. He moved in beside Mr. Darby, put a hand on the window, and stared out. The City of Species that he knew was gone. The streets were in shadow, a dense, dark fog hanging over everything. Animals lumbered around, their eyes glowing red and patches of fur missing. Some were fighting in the street, clawing and biting one another. They reminded Noah of the sasquatches and what the Shadowist had done to them.

When a few fireflies flashed beside Noah, a grizzly bear turned its gaze toward the window. Noah looked into the beast's red eyes and gasped.

"Don't worry," Mr. Darby said. "The glass is tinted to protect the artwork. We're perfectly hidden."

As the grizzly stalked over to the glass, Noah realized it was seeing its reflection. Thick drool dangled from its black lip, and its long claws etched lines in the street. It slowly swung its head from side to side and growled, probably thinking its image was another bear. As it got within a few feet of the museum, it fell back on its haunches and swung

100

one of its front legs, just missing the glass. Then it abruptly turned and ran off, its paws pounding the street and its muscles quaking.

"It doesn't know that it's sick," Mr. Darby said. "None of the animals do."

Noah looked out at the lions, giraffes, rhinos, and tigers. They looked like monsters, not animals.

"They'll flood your streets, Noah," Mr. Darby solemnly said. "If we can't stop them, they'll use the portals—old and new—to attack your world. It could happen at any moment. Tonight, perhaps."

Noah stared out at the dark city and imagined Clarksville looking the same way. "There are people I can go to for help," he said. "My parents. The police. The *army*."

Mr. Darby shook his head. "That might be what DeGraff wants."

Noah turned his attention to the old man. A firefly touched down in his beard, flashed once, and then flew off again. "What are you talking about?"

"The clouds," Mr. Darby said, gesturing out the window toward the dark sky. "Their shadows are full of DeGraff's magic. What if he were to release a storm on your police? Your armies?"

The thought peaked Noah's fear. He considered how Charlie Red and the other security guards had been changed by DeGraff's magic. Then he imagined the armies of Earth under the Shadowist's command.

"No," Mr. Darby said. "We'll have to do it ourselves." He pointed to a tall tower that was barely visible in the fog. "There. Teknikal Tower. Our Teknikals made it back to their base. They're hard at work on the Multipoint Portal."

"How close are they?"

"Close."

Noah stared at Teknikal Tower. Zak, a weird, wily teenager with bad hair and hygiene, was the world's best hope.

"Did you come upstairs for the truth?" Mr. Darby asked.

Noah nodded.

Mr. Darby walked off, saying, "Let's go, then, shall we?"

Noah hesitated. He watched the old man through the flashing fireflies. His heart started to race as he began to feel unsure about whether he wanted to hear what Mr. Darby had to say. On his shoulder, Marlo chirped, and Noah glanced over to meet the kingfisher's beady-eyed gaze.

"Okay," Noah said to Marlo. "We'll go."

He steadied Tameron's backpack, *his* backpack, and hurried after the man who still seemed to have his greatest secret to tell.

CHAPTER 11

ACROSS THE INSTITUTE OF LIGHT

As Mr. Darby led Noah across the museum, he said, "I suppose you're wondering about the fireflies—why they're here, and why there are so many."

Noah nodded even though fireflies inhabiting a building seemed ordinary enough for the Secret Zoo.

Mr. Darby gestured to the surrounding artwork. "The natural light from the fireflies doesn't damage the art."

Noah gently brushed a few fireflies off his arm, saying, "So that's why it's called the Institute of Light."

"Partly," Mr. Darby said. "But mostly the name refers to the illuminating quality of art."

The old man led them to a new wing of the museum, pushing through a pair of unlocked doors. Here, the artwork showed the buildings of the City of Species in various states of construction. In some of the art, animals were helping, pulling carts full of supplies and carrying construction workers on their backs. In one painting, dozens of monkeys were scaling the tall steel framework of a new building to take tools to workers in the heights. "Our history," Mr. Darby said as he gestured around him. "And our future, I hope."

Mr. Darby paused and leaned over a drinking fountain. He held back his bushy beard with one hand and put his lips to the stream of water. Then he stood up straight, gave a loud *"Aaahhh..."* and continued walking, his hands once again clasped behind his back.

Noah grinned. Mr. Darby was like a kid in so many ways, playful and impulsive. How many men would pause to sip from a drinking fountain and then so loudly express their pleasure? Mr. Darby—an old man who wore a flashy velvet jacket and knew all the animals in his world by name. Sometimes he hardly seemed real. Sometimes he felt like a character from a daydream.

As they entered a new hall, they walked through groupings of fireflies like patches of magical, blinking snow. Above an open doorway, a sign read THE HISTORY OF THE SECRET ZOO, and Noah followed Mr. Darby into the respective room, a small gallery filled with art and artifacts. As Mr. Darby walked along a wall covered with old black-and-white photographs, he stopped and pointed to a grainy picture of a small town on a quiet street. Noah saw a barbershop with a striped pole and a sturdy-looking church with a tall steeple.

"Clarksville," he said. "Early days." He moved to a new photograph, another black-and-white shot of a stately home with large columns. "The Jackson House. My house." He pointed to a window on the second story. "This was Frederick's room." He smiled a sad smile and took a step away; almost reluctantly, it seemed.

The next picture showed an old farmhouse with loose shutters and a crooked porch. Beneath the picture, words were engraved on a shiny gold plate. Noah leaned in and read them.

WHERE SIMON THE SIMIAN CAME FROM.
SIMON BECAME THE FIRST ANIMAL IN MR.
JACKSON'S PRIVATE ZOO.

The farmhouse was exactly like Noah had imagined it while sitting on the floor of Hummingbird Hideout, listening to the story of Simon for the first time.

Mr. Darby started walking again, pointing out the photographs, most of which were animals. A white fox, four ferrets, a peacock, a crocodile, and a chimpanzee. They came to a picture of a monkey with messy gray fur, long limbs, and a winding tail. A langur. Simon. Noah could practically see him jumping across the furniture in the Jackson house.

"The first cage," Mr. Darby said. He was now pointing to a display case toward the middle of the room. In it was a series of rusty steel rails. "Or what's left of it, anyway. I still remember building it."

"For Simon?" Noah asked.

Mr. Darby nodded. "Once it became clear I couldn't keep the animals in my house, I had no other choice." He stared at what remained of Simon's cage. "I tried to make them as large and comfortable as I could, but you can't re-create the places animals long to be." He walked over to another picture on the wall and softly tapped the glass. "It was a lesson this kind boy learned, as well."

Noah moved to see who Mr. Darby was talking about: a smiling boy with rounded features and adult teeth that seemed too big for his mouth. His cheeks were dotted with soft freckles, and his messy hair stood up in different directions. Frederick.

"My boy." Mr. Darby forced a smile and tried to hide his pain. "I still miss him." He reached into his pocket and pulled out the photograph Noah had seen him holding. Then he showed Noah. Another picture of Frederick.

Noah touched the old man's shoulder to let him know he wasn't as alone as he probably felt. Mr. Darby continued to force a smile. Fireflies reflected in the dark lenses of his sunglasses, and again Noah briefly wondered about his eyes.

"You should have told us that you're Mr. Jackson," Noah said.

"I didn't want to scare you."

"So your jacket keeps you alive—that's not so scary."

"The jacket does more than that. It defines me. Mr. Darby, I mean."

106

Noah raised an eyebrow.

Mr. Darby started to walk off again, saying, "Come. Let me show you something else."

As they headed to the other side of the gallery, fireflies landed on their clothes and blinked like tiny white bulbs on a Christmas tree. Noah ducked and dodged the winged insects. Mr. Darby stopped at a tall rectangular glass case where a large piece of fabric was on display. Noah realized it was a curtain—dull red with fabric like old velvet. He moved in beside Mr. Darby and read the engraving on a small plate attached to the cabinet.

MR. DARBY'S FIRST JACKET

"Jacket?" Noah said. "But it's a curtain."

"Only at first glance," Mr. Darby said. "Or perhaps to those who lack imagination. Frederick never did. And after his mother died, he more or less vacated our world in favor of the ones in his head. I sometimes wonder if he kept his mother alive there."

Mr. Darby became quiet. He stared at the curtain, which seemed like a screen for the movie of his memories to play upon.

"The animals—oh, he loved the animals! First Simon, then the others. He spent hours playing with them from outside their cages, creating games and imagining things.

They cured his depression, but not mine." Mr. Darby became quiet. He smiled, frowned, and smiled again. "I tried over and over to reach out to my son, to bridge the distance between us. For a long time, I couldn't. But then…I found a way."

Mr. Darby—the man who was really Mr. Jackson, Frederick's father—took a step forward and put a hand on the glass cabinet. Then he took a deep breath and began to tell the final part of his tale.

CHAPTER 12

THE FIRST PORTAL

My boy, Frederick, sitting in our backyard, reaching through the steel bars of the cages to pet the animals and let them eat from his hands. And me at the window of our house, hiding and watching through an opening between the curtains. All of it is too familiar.

I long to go out to him—to run through the back door and scoop him up in my arms and hold his body against mine. But it seems impossible now. The distance between us has grown too big.

Frederick fixes a button on his zookeeper costume—something he wears when he imagines his worlds—walks over to a new cage, and kneels in front of it. This animal is his favorite. Simon. The monkey from the old farmhouse. The first animal in our private zoo. I don't know Simon is my son's favorite because Frederick has told me; I know from watching. This is what my role as a father has been reduced to. Watching.

Simon, playful as always, jumps to the front of his cage and sniffs Frederick's hand. Then he turns and allows the boy to gently stroke his back. The monkey, like me, longs for Frederick's touch.

Go to him, a voice inside me says. *He's your son. Things can be better again.*

Though the voice sounds like mine, I know whose it really is. My wife's—Frederick's mother. She still talks to me.

"I can't," I say, surprised by the sound of my voice, something that's rarely heard in the Jackson house.

You can, my wife says. *Go. He wants you to. But he's a boy, and boys don't know how to say these things. You're the adult—you're the father.*

I glance back at the window—Frederick has moved out of sight. I grab one of the pleated curtains and pull it back for a better view. Frederick has moved to a new spot and is reaching again into Simon's cage, pretending to want to grab the monkey's long tail. Then he adjusts the collar on his costume.

Go to him—just play with him. You can be his father another day.

Yes. This makes sense: to be his father another day. *I* cannot go to him, but someone else can—someone who's willing to participate in Frederick's zookeeper game.

I pull the curtain back a bit more for a better look at my son; the fabric is as smooth as velvet.

An idea strikes me, and before I have the sense to stop myself, I pull on the curtain, hard. One of the gold rings that

110

attaches the fabric to the overhead rod snaps, falls to the ground, and rolls to a stop a few feet away. I tighten my grasp and pull again, harder than before. This time, two rings break free and clatter on the tile.

I gaze out the window. Frederick seems a million miles away, lost in whatever world he's created to deal with his pain. A lost mother, a lost father. Maybe I can correct the second thing.

Tink! Tink! Two more rings strike the floor.

I gaze up. One ring left. A final tug and the curtain is free.

I heave the curtain onto my back and square it across my shoulders, surprised by the weight. It hangs across my body like the robe of a king. I pick up a gold ring and force it to pierce both sides of the fabric just below my neck—a clasp to hold the pretend robe in place. I reach for the door and quickly turn the knob before I have time to think. As I head across the backyard, my walk becomes a stride, and I begin to imagine myself as somebody new. Then I stop and stand behind Frederick.

"Ahem."

Frederick turns at the sound, sees me, and falls out of his squat. He gazes up with wide eyes. "Dad?" he says, and to hear my name in his voice warms my heart. How long has it been since he's called me that?

But I am not Dad, not today. I'm someone else,

someone standing on the verge of Frederick's daydreams.

"I'm afraid not, dear boy," I say in a voice that is not quite my own. "May I ask your name?"

Frederick doesn't answer right away, and for one terrible moment I fear he won't allow me to participate in his story. Then the hard look on his face softens and he says, "Frederick."

"Fred-er-ick," I say, tasting each syllable. "Do you frequently travel these parts?"

"Dad," he says, "what are you—"

I squat beside my son before he can come too close to reality. I realize I don't know how to play his game, so I give him the lead.

"What's this creature's name?" I say, pointing at Simon.

Frederick thinks about it, and then says, "Simon."

"What a grand name! Simon! Simon the Simian!"

The person I'm pretending to be isn't quite clear to me. Perhaps he's inspired by someone I've read about in a novel or seen in the theater. Or maybe he's little pieces of everyone I've ever met and accidentally remembered.

"Why the cage, dear boy?" I gesture to the trees in our lavish backyard. "Why not let him free?"

Frederick shrugs. "Rules."

"Rulers?"

Frederick shakes his head as he strokes Simon's side.

The monkey is standing at the front of his cage, studying me. "No...*rules*. Laws."

"Ahhh..." I say. "Most *constricting* things."

Frederick smiles. What ten-year-old boy doesn't hate rules?

I reach my arm out toward the cage. "May I?"

Frederick shrugs—the closest I'll get to an invitation. As I squat beside the cage, my makeshift robe spreads out on the ground around me. I hold up my palm to show Simon I don't have anything, and then I reach into the cage. His hair is soft and smooth, and I understand for the first time why Frederick likes to touch it.

"Will he bite?" I ask.

"No," Frederick says. "Never."

"Then why not get closer?"

Frederick looks at me, confused.

"The cage—why not go into the cage?"

"My dad. He won't—" He stares at me again and seems to remember who I really am. Then he continues anyway. "He won't let me."

"Oh? Is he afraid of the animals?"

Frederick shrugs. "He's afraid of a lot of things."

His words hurt, but I pretend they don't. "Well...your father's not here right now. Should we go into the cage?"

"How?" Frederick asks. "It's locked."

"Let me see what I can do about that!" I stand and turn

113

my back to Frederick so he can't see me reach into my pocket and take a key off my key ring. I face Frederick again, saying, "This should work nicely."

"What is it?" Frederick asks. I realize that a part of him believes all this is really happening, and I remember how liberating a child's imagination can be.

"A magic key," I say, holding it up. "It will work in any lock here." The second part is true. I'm holding a skeleton key; it's designed to fit the locks on all my cages.

Frederick stands and then hesitates. He isn't sure about something.

"Come!" I say, turning and heading for the door of the cage.

Frederick follows. Seconds later, the key fits neatly, the lock loudly clicks, and the steel door swings open.

"Inside!" I say. "Quick!"

Frederick hurries into the cage, and I close the door behind us. His broad smile warms my heart. It's the first time I've been this close to my son in years.

Simon pounces over to us. He glances up at me and begins to sniff the curtain on my back.

"Curious creature," I say. "It might serve us to—"

I lose my voice. Simon has crawled up the curtain and is now standing across my shoulders, his body pressed against the back of my head.

"Whoa!" I say, and this time it's my genuine voice.

114

But Frederick is laughing—*laughing*—and there's no way I can turn back now.

"Aggressive rascal, isn't he?" I've never used the word "rascal" in my life, but that doesn't matter to the person I'm pretending to be.

Frederick claps as Simon turns around, briefly placing his hand on my head and swatting my face with his long tail.

"Indeed! Indeed!" I say in my new, loud voice.

"What's your name?" Frederick asks.

For a second I don't know who he's talking to. Then I remember that Frederick's father is not in the cage—not really.

"My name?" I panic because I don't have one, and any hesitation on something as simple as this might draw Frederick out of our game, which is feeling more and more like a place I want to be. I glance at my pretend robe. The edge of one side is folded over, and I can see a tag that reads DARBY DRAPES.

"Why...I'm Mr. Darby," I say.

Frederick smiles more than ever, and I see right away that Mr. Darby is going to become the friend that Frederick has been missing.

"Let me pet him," Frederick says.

I squat, careful not to lose my balance. Frederick reaches up and strokes Simon's back.

As much as a minute passes without a word between us.

I become concerned when I see that Frederick has lost his smile.

"Sometimes I worry about the animals," Frederick says. I'm not sure if he's talking to me or Mr. Darby. Perhaps both.

"Oh?" I say, careful not to lose the unique voice that's growing inside me.

Frederick nods. "It's not normal to have animals like this in your backyard. Like I said…there are rules. I hear people talking about them."

He's referring to the gossip—I know because I've heard it, too. *It's filthy. The animals carry disease. You can't keep pets like that in Clarksville.* The newspaper even printed an article against my private zoo.

I see something in Frederick's face then. Pain—real pain. The kind that lingers after tragically losing someone you love. The kind that comes from wondering if you could have done something to prevent it. I know this pain because I've felt it myself.

I reach out and hold my son's shoulder and realize there is power in my grip—not because I'm a man, but because I'm a father.

"Don't worry," I say—or rather, Mr. Darby says. "I'll keep your animals safe. Forever."

CHAPTER 13

CHAIN REACTION

After sharing his memories, Mr. Darby was quiet for a long time. He continued to stare at the ratty curtain hanging in the display cabinet, the portal into his past. He finally turned his attention back to Noah.

Noah tried to speak but couldn't. His words seemed tangled in his emotions. All around them, fireflies continued to blink.

"Grab one," Mr. Darby said.

"Huh?"

"The fireflies. Grab one and hold it for a few seconds."

It seemed a strange thing to say after telling such an emotional story, but sometimes Mr. Darby was like that. He never wanted people to stay in a painful place for long.

Noah snatched a firefly out of the air and held it in his hand, his fingertips facing up. He glanced at Mr. Darby when nothing happened.

"Wait," Mr. Darby said. "It only takes a moment."

Light started to seep out around Noah's fingers. Then he felt warmth against his skin. The light grew brighter and brighter, and then produced a heat that was too much to bear.

Noah opened his fingers, and his hand seemed to burst with light. Other nearby fireflies began to glow intensely bright, and then more and more—a chain reaction working outward. Noah, squinting, held his arms up like a shield. Hundreds of fireflies followed suit, and then the light in the room slowly dimmed back to normal.

"Whoa…" Noah said. "What was *that*?"

"A defense mechanism," Mr. Darby said. "Something they've learned to do. Fireflies don't like to be caught and put in glass jars. You might spread the news to the children in your world."

Noah nodded and watched the firefly he'd caught drift off.

A few seconds passed in silence. Noah wanted to ask Mr. Darby about his story, but he didn't want to risk wiping away the smile that had found its way back onto the man's face. Still, he couldn't contain his curiosity for long: "Your eyes…does your jacket…"

"Yes," Mr. Darby said. "The magic provides what my natural body no longer can. Sight, in this case."

Noah shook his head, almost unable to believe it.

"The Secret Zoo needs me," Mr. Darby said. "I never thought I'd stay this long, but I can't just leave, not with DeGraff on the loose."

DeGraff. The Shadowist. Noah suddenly realized something.

118

"You met him," Noah said.

"Excuse me?"

"DeGraff—*Mr.* DeGraff—you met him when this first began. He came to your door—Mr. Jackson's door. It was after Frederick died. He came to your house and told you how to create the Secret Zoo."

Mr. Darby slowly nodded. "He was hardly the Shadowist then. Just an ordinary man with a vendetta against the world. Since then, dark magic has ravaged him and made him the monster he is today."

"He used you. Your wealth…all your resources. He used you to bring the magic to America."

"And the animals," Mr. Darby said. "He knew of the Secret Society, how it was scattered in groups around the world, and he knew the type of army he could build."

"But how did he know you'd help him?"

Mr. Darby raised the back of his hand to allow a firefly to touch down on him. The firefly nestled its wings and then flashed once, twice.

"The story of my private zoo was big news. DeGraff came to Clarksville—he came to my home and saw something other than the animals. He saw opportunity. He realized what the animals meant to Frederick, and what Frederick meant to me." Mr. Darby frowned and became quiet for what seemed a very long time. He blew the firefly off his hand with a quick outward breath and then pressed

119

his palms together. "That was when DeGraff did the unthinkable." Mr. Darby turned his head and stared off into an empty part of the room. "Frederick. DeGraff poisoned him. He poisoned him, knowing that it would ruin me."

Noah felt his heart drop. "But I thought…You told us Frederick died in his sleep and the doctors couldn't figure out why."

"The first part was true," Mr. Darby said. "The second part was a lie. The doctors not only knew how Frederick died, but I was a suspect in the investigation of his death."

"How…how could they think that?"

Mr. Darby stared at the old curtain in the display cabinet as if trying to find a memory there. "People…they thought I'd lost my mind. The animals in my yard, me dressing as Mr. Darby—all signs of my madness, they claimed, brought on by my wife's tragic death."

Mr. Darby looked back at Noah, and Noah thought of the old man's eyes, murky and white. He wished he could see them—wished that Mr. Darby wouldn't hide behind his dark glasses.

"In the end, I was acquitted, but I was never truly allowed to go free. My wealth, my power—people saw these things as the reason I was never brought to justice."

Noah shook his head in disbelief.

"I was cast out by my community. I stayed indoors, alone in the empty mansion. And then I *did* go mad, slowly.

120

The ghosts of my wife and Frederick haunted me—not as spirits, but as thoughts and memories, things that came alive in the endless halls of my home, a place that had become a prison."

Mr. Darby reached up and touched his cheek, and Noah realized he'd wiped away a tear.

"Mr. Jackson slowly died, bit by bit. I wanted him gone. I found myself wearing the robe all the time, and spending my days with the animals. I cared for them endlessly, and knew them all by name.

"That was when DeGraff seized the opportunity he'd created. He came to me with stories of Bhanu and his magic. I went to India and learned about the zoo I could build—another world just beyond my back door, a place where all of Frederick's beloved animals could be safe...and a place where Mr. Darby could be free."

Noah could barely believe what he was hearing. He just stood and stared. Bright light began to glow from a place in his jacket, and he realized a firefly had gotten trapped in his pocket. He let it free.

"They'll do that sometimes," Mr. Darby said with a smile that was clearly forced. "They get into a tight place, get comfortable, and can't find their way out."

Noah watched the firefly go, glad for the distraction. A few fireflies near it briefly shined bright—a small chain reaction like the other Noah had seen.

"You should go home, Noah," Mr. Darby said. Then he led the way out of the gallery. Noah, his head full of Mr. Darby's incredible past, barely noticed the artwork and the fireflies. All he saw were images in his head: the cages in Mr. Darby's backyard; DeGraff standing on Mr. Darby's porch; magic and machines slowly bringing the Secret Zoo to life. Then, when Noah came to the exit of the room, a framed photograph caught his eye. When he stopped walking to take a better look, so did Mr. Darby. The black-and-white picture showed a tombstone bearing the names of Mr. Jackson, his wife, and his son. Mr. Jackson's name was the only one without a date for a death.

"It's in Clarksville Cemetery," Mr. Darby explained.

Noah nodded. He knew the place, an old cemetery just outside his neighborhood.

Mr. Darby touched his fingertips to the glass. He smiled in a sad way and said, "A place I think I belong."

Noah wanted to say something, but couldn't find the right words.

"Come," Mr. Darby said as he lowered his hand. He turned and headed out the door, adding, "Let's go."

They walked through the gentle firefly storm and then stopped at the staircase to the basement. Mr. Darby said, "You can find your way from here, yes?"

Noah nodded. After descending a few stairs, he turned and said, "Mr. Darby?"

122

The old man stared at Noah, firefly light reflecting in the dark lenses of his glasses. "Yes?"

"I'm…I'm sorry. For all that happened. To you."

"Thank you, Noah," Mr. Darby said. "But the time for sorrow is behind us. Now is the time to protect the Secret Zoo, once and for all."

His powerful words reminded Noah of a king's decree. And this thought brought on a memory.

"The Descenders…outside Creepy Critters…why did they kneel to you?"

The leader of the Secret Zoo smiled a weak smile. For a few seconds, it seemed that he wouldn't answer, but then he said, "I'll keep some secrets. At least for now."

Noah wanted to ask more, but Mr. Darby was already walking off, fireflies jumping out from the folds in his jacket and flashing in the air. He rounded a corner and was gone.

"You get what you needed?" someone asked.

Noah turned and saw Sam standing at the bottom of the stairs. Noah considered the question and nodded, but without much conviction.

"Good," Sam said. He started to leave, saying, "Let's get you home."

Home. Noah wondered how much longer he'd be able to call it that if DeGraff succeeded. Then he ran down the stairs, trying to escape the answer that scared him most.

CHAPTER 14

THE CAPTURE

As soon as Noah walked through the portal into his closet, a loud squeal erupted in his ear, and he yanked out his headset. Sam did the same. Someone was jamming the radio waves. Marlo, who'd been on Noah's shoulder, flew into the main part of the bedroom and touched down on the windowsill. Before Noah could react, Sam grabbed his arm and ordered him to be quiet.

They crept out into the bedroom. Noah's heart dropped when he saw that dim light from the first floor was filling the upstairs hall.

"Sam?" Noah whispered.

"I see."

Noah turned his attention to his bed—the mirage wasn't working. The chameleons were gone, and so was the pile of clothes he'd stuffed beneath his covers. He took a step toward the door, but Sam grabbed his arm, stopping him again. The two stared out into the dimly lit hall, listening for sounds. After a few seconds, Noah heard something— footsteps, coming from downstairs.

Noah flinched as something ran across his foot. He

looked down and saw a chameleon—one from the mirage—crawl beneath his bed.

"Follow me," Sam whispered. The Descender slowly walked across the room. At the door, more sounds came from downstairs—floorboards creaking in the kitchen, and a low growl, like that of a distant animal. Noah could smell something that didn't belong—the pungent, earthy odor of the air after a storm, and of things that have gotten wet. And something else. Noah thought for a few seconds and then realized what it was. Disease.

Sam got Noah's attention and pointed to a firefly on Noah's shoulder. Then he grabbed the winged insect before its light could shine and gently placed it in a pocket in Noah's jacket. Noah nodded and then buttoned the pocket.

Sam led the way into the hall, his footsteps slow and cautious. When the two reached Megan's room and faced her open door, panic washed over Noah. The dim moonlight revealed that Megan's dresser was turned over, and her bedsheets were lying on the floor. The mirror above her desk was shattered, and moonlight was reflecting off the shards of glass.

"No," Noah said, and he took a step away from the scene. The room started to spin, and Sam squeezed his arm, hard. In another time, at another place, it might have hurt, but now Noah barely felt it. His fear spiked as he thought of his parents. He pulled away from Sam, turned, and took two steps into the room on the other side of the hall. More signs of a struggle: an overturned desk, and books lying open on the carpet. His mother and father were gone.

"This…this is our fault!" Noah said. "Sam—we should have been here!"

Again, Noah noticed the strange smell of moist earth and sickness. He heard another distant grunt, and then something else—a faint caw, like that of a large bird.

Something was downstairs.

"Noah," Sam said, "keep quiet. We don't—"

Noah's attention went to another sound—footsteps on the stairs. Before he could warn Sam, someone slammed into the Descender and drove him down the hall, out of sight. Then the house shook as the two bodies slammed into the wall. The sounds of the fight were amplified in the tight confines of the hallway, and then there was silence.

Noah stood in his parents' room and stared out into his limited view of the hall, all his attention on the silence, which seemed to stretch on and on. "Sam?" he eventually uttered.

A nearby floorboard groaned and someone stepped into the open doorway, a man with long, lanky arms and a messy mop of hair. Though his face was hidden in shadow, Noah could tell who it was. Charlie Red.

Something swooped down and struck Charlie's neck. Marlo. When the kingfisher attacked a second time, Charlie

126

batted him away.

"Marlo!" Noah called out.

Charlie smiled a wicked smile. Then he pounced on Noah, put him in a headlock, and pulled him out of the room. As Noah was dragged down the hall, he saw Sam lying on the floor, seemingly unconscious, and Marlo struggling to fly. Noah's heels banged down the steps, and then Charlie threw him to the floor of the living room. Air gushed out of Noah's chest, and his side erupted in pain as he was kicked once, twice, three times. He rolled onto his stomach and tried to crawl away.

"Where you going?" Charlie said.

Charlie's foot connected with Noah's knee, and fresh pain erupted in his leg. As Noah spun onto his back, the bottom of Charlie's foot came down on his throat, and the air of the world was suddenly a million miles away. Noah felt something wedged between him and the ground and realized it was the backpack—he was still wearing it. He immediately pulled the cords in his shoulder straps and the tail sprang out of the pack, catapulting Noah into the air and knocking over Charlie Red.

Noah stumbled and leaned against a wall for support, his breath coming in gasps. He smelled the earthy smell, stronger than ever. And then he felt something—wind. He looked into the kitchen and saw where these things were coming from: a portal in the outside wall of his house. Wind from the Secret Zoo was blowing the curtain around, revealing glimpses of the City of Species—dark and stormy, just like Noah had seen from the window in the Institute of Light. DeGraff had built another portal to Noah's house.

As Noah turned to face Charlie, his tail dragged along the floor and whacked the wall behind him. Objects fell and shattered—the knickknacks Mr. Darby had used in his example of the Multipoint. Charlie stood in the dim light, and Noah realized something horrifying about the zoo security guard. He was taller than ever, and his arms were freakishly long, his hands dangling down by his knees. DeGraff's magic was continuing to change Charlie, just like the sasquatches and the other animals.

"Why are you doing this?" Noah said, still gasping for air.

"The world has lost order, kid. It needs a new king—a new way of thinking."

"DeGraff's a lunatic!" Noah said. "He ruined Mr. Darby!"

"You mean Mr. Jackson?" Charlie said, and Noah could see his smile. "Poor, poor Frederick. And only a boy. But look on the bright side—his mother wasn't around to miss him."

Noah balled his hands into fists. He wanted to lash out at Charlie Red, to strike and fight, like a Descender.

"They'll all die, of course," Charlie said. "Your friends,

I mean. Those who refuse to"—he raised his sickeningly long arms into the light—"*change*. Your sister, that stubborn brat, she'll certainly be one of them."

"We'll *beat* you!" Noah said. "We'll fight, and in the end—"

"The end? You mean tonight at midnight?"

Noah stared at Charlie, unsure what to think. Then he glanced at a clock and saw it was already 10:27.

Charlie noticed his interest and said, "Go ahead—set your watch, kid. We storm your world at exactly twelve o'clock."

"You're…you're lying. Why would you tell me?"

"To watch you *squirm*, kid," Charlie answered. "There's nothing you can do to stop us."

Noah exploded with rage. He swung his tail like he had in the Institute of Light, and it dragged along the wall, crushing the plaster. Charlie ducked and the tail passed over his head and smashed an armoire to pieces. Noah whipped his tail back around, this time connecting with Charlie and batting him across the room. Charlie rolled, jumped to his feet, and faced Noah again. Drywall dust swirled in the dim light.

"You took my parents!" Noah shouted. "My sister!"

Charlie glanced at the curtain, which was still blowing around as wind from another world forced its way into Noah's kitchen.

"We were disappointed not to find you here, kid. But we're glad to see you back."

We. Charlie wasn't alone. And just as Noah had this thought, three people stepped through the portal—three hulking figures, silhouettes in the dark kitchen. They lumbered over to Noah, their hands swinging by their knees. These were the men, Noah realized, who had dragged his family into the City of Species. Now they were coming for him.

Noah turned and attacked, but his tail became wedged against the wall. The three men pounced on him.

"The backpack—get his backpack!"

Noah, still standing, was yanked one way, and then another. Someone pulled the cords in his shoulder straps, and his tail slammed against him as it retracted into his pack. Then his Descender gear was stripped away.

"Hold him!" Charlie said.

"We're trying!" one of his attackers called out in a deep, throaty voice—the monstrous voice of a creature that was no longer quite human.

Noah felt the crook of an arm press against his throat as he was put in another headlock. A fist connected with his stomach, and the air rushed out of him. He wheezed as he took a breath. Then he stopped fighting before another blow could come.

Charlie's shadow moved across the floor. His

unnaturally long, lanky frame made him look like a comic book villain.

Just then, the curtain opened and someone walked into Noah's world. DeGraff. He moved across the kitchen, his long trench coat beating against his heels and blowing around like a cape. He stopped directly beside Noah, his face just inches away, and Noah felt his warm, moist breath on his cheeks.

"Hello, boy." His voice rumbled in his throat, revealing again how his fleshy insides were decaying. "You got the other one, right?" DeGraff said to Charlie. "The girl?"

Charlie nodded. "And a couple bonuses. His parents. They got in the way."

The idea of Charlie putting his filthy hands on Noah's mother and father, dragging them across the floor, sickened Noah. He struggled to get loose from his captors, but it was no use.

Noah turned his attention back to DeGraff and saw the horrific details of his face. His missing nose and top lip. His black gum line and broken teeth. The empty sockets of his eyes. DeGraff—a creature from a nightmare.

"Are you scared, boy?" DeGraff asked.

"No," Noah said, but the lie was obvious. "You won't win—not in the end."

"I always win. Ask your friend, the old man."

"Mr. Darby's stronger than you think!" Noah said.

"Look at him—he built the Secret Zoo!"

"No, boy," DeGraff said. "*I* built the Secret Zoo. Darby was my pawn. And so was his child."

Noah filled with new anger. He imagined Frederick's chubby cheeks and warm eyes—a boy brought to life in Mr. Darby's stories. He thought of Frederick's good heart, his compassion for the animals. If Noah had been born a hundred years ago, the two of them might have been friends.

"You killed him!" Noah said.

"People die all the time. For different reasons."

Noah continued to shake his head. "You're...you're *sick*! Evil!"

DeGraff chuckled, and it was a nauseating sound—a gurgle of watery phlegm. "I'm a leader, boy. Leaders understand the necessity of sacrifice, even when it's the life of a child."

Noah shook his head again. How could someone believe such a thing?

"And speaking of sacrifice..." DeGraff said.

He nodded toward the three men, and a second later Noah's legs were swept out from beneath him, and he fell to the floor.

"Take him to his family," the Shadowist said as he stepped aside to clear a path to the curtain.

Two of the men grabbed Noah's ankles and began to pull him along the floor. Noah, on his back, reached out and grabbed a leg of the couch. He needed to get to his family, but not like this—not without the help of Mr. Darby and the Descenders. His hand slipped off the couch, and then his body banged against the frame of the open doorway to the kitchen.

Do something! a voice inside him said. *Do something or you and your family are finished!*

He felt a cold breeze, and he looked to see the curtain flapping in the wind from the City of Species—a dark, dreary place that had once been filled with color and movement and a better magic. A place that had once been filled with hope and light.

His thoughts stopped. Light. He remembered the firefly Sam had caught upstairs, and he remembered the way the light had hurt DeGraff in the Secret Chamber of Lights. As he was dragged along, he unbuttoned his jacket pocket and softly closed his hand around the still-captive insect.

Hold it, the voice inside him said. *Hold it for as long as you can.*

The curtain was barely ten feet away. Knowing he needed time for the light to build, he reached out with his free hand and grabbed a leg of the kitchen table. He stopped sliding for a few seconds. Then the men holding him realized what was happening and pulled him away.

The heat against his palm grew more and more intense. It felt like he was holding the tip of a match.

He was dragged closer and closer to the portal—eight feet, seven feet, six. The curtain continued to flap open, revealing the red eyes of the animals on the streets. Someone started to laugh, and Noah knew by the sick sound that it was DeGraff.

He checked his hand, saw light seeping out from between his fingers, and hoped no one would notice.

Don't let go. Accept the pain. And then his inner voice said something that surprised him: *Pain is part of what makes a Descender strong.*

But he wasn't a Descender. At least not yet.

Just as the men who were dragging Noah were about to step through the portal, the curtain swept open and a large animal flew into the room, plowing into the men and knocking them over. The animal lost control, struck the floor, and slid into the dim light, revealing there were actually two animals. One was a penguin—a large emperor penguin. Podgy. And then Noah realized the second figure wasn't an animal at all. It was a young girl with pigtails and eyeglasses that somehow hadn't fallen off in the crash. Megan.

Noah, free from the clutches of the men, jumped to his feet. The pain in his hand was worse than ever, but he needed to hold on longer. He only had one firefly, and only one chance to make this work.

"Get them!" DeGraff commanded. "All of them!"

134

The men stood, looked at Podgy, and seemed to register what had just happened. Megan and Podgy moved behind the kitchen table.

One of the men pointed to Noah and said, "His hand! What's wrong with his hand?"

Noah looked down. His fingers were glowing orange.

"Meg!" Noah said. "Close your eyes!"

"*Hurry—get them!*" DeGraff bellowed, his panicky voice gurgling out of his throat.

The three men charged—two at Podgy and Megan, and one at Noah. Noah swiftly raised his arm and uncurled his fingers, and a blinding burst of white light filled the room. As Noah closed his eyes, he heard Charlie, the men, and DeGraff howl in pain.

An idea struck him. Someone had jammed the radio waves, but there were other ways to communicate with the Crossers. With his eyes still closed, he ran into the living room, his arms out in front of him, his hands feeling the way. Something soft touched his fingers—the drapes over the large window in the front of his house. He quickly threw them open, allowing the bright light to spill out onto his street.

Someone suddenly tackled him, and when Noah struck the floor, he instinctively opened his eyes. The firefly was already dimming. Noah could make out the walls, the ceiling, a chandelier—and Charlie Red hovering over him.

"I got him!" Charlie said.

"Just kill him!" DeGraff instructed.

"With pleasure."

Noah noticed something. The freckles on Charlie's face weren't so splotchy, and his eyes had lost their redness. Then, when Charlie tried to grab Noah, they were both shocked when his hands didn't reach. Somehow his arms weren't so supernaturally long.

Charlie glanced at his hands, confused. Then he arched his back and howled in pain. Noah didn't understand until he looked past Charlie and saw Solana standing at the open front door with her right hand down by her left knee. She'd just pitched a handful of quills into Charlie's back.

Hannah squeezed past Solana. Then a second Descender, a third—more and more. The Descenders on patrol were responding to the bright light, Noah's call for help.

Charlie ran from the room and into the kitchen. Noah didn't have to see him to know where he was going—the portal to the Secret Zoo. The Descenders rushed after him. Seconds later, a Descender stepped back into the living room, saying, "He's gone."

"There were others," Noah said. "DeGraff."

"Gone too," the Descender said. He looked at Hannah and asked, "Should we go after them?"

"Don't!" Megan said. "Not yet. They might be waiting

on the other side—another trap!"

Hannah considered the situation for a few seconds and then shook her head. "Get Mr. Darby. Take the portal in Noah's room."

The Descender nodded. Then he rushed up the stairs and was gone.

Noah closed his eyes and softly shook his head. DeGraff had escaped, again. And this time, he'd taken Noah's parents.

CHAPTER 15

THE MODS

"Here," Solana said, "wrap it in this."

Noah took the damp hand towel she held out to him and wrapped it around the red, blistering wound in the palm of his hand. Solana sat beside Noah, and the two leaned against his living room wall.

"How bad is it?" someone asked.

Noah looked up and saw Mr. Darby, who had just been retrieved from the Institute of Light.

"Not bad," Noah said.

Solana shook her head. "It's bad."

Noah looked around and saw the people and animals gathered around him—some had come off Perimeter Patrol, and some had come from the Institute of Light. He saw Specters, Descenders, prairie dogs, and Podgy. Someone had retrieved Blizzard from the shed, and now the polar bear was stretched out across the living room, his big head resting in Noah's lap. Sam, conscious again, was standing and leaning against the wall for support.

A large black box with rows of knobs, buttons, and dials sat in one corner of the room. An RF Jammer, a device that blocked radio frequencies. Charlie or one of his goons had brought it, and it was why Noah's headset hadn't worked. As soon as the RF Jammer was turned off, Noah had used his headset to check on Ella and Richie and was relieved to find out that they hadn't been attacked. Noah briefed them on what had happened and then told them—and Evie and Tank—to be on high alert.

Now Noah craned his neck to try to see through the doorway into the kitchen.

"Can you see?" Mr. Darby asked.

Noah shook his head.

"Lee-Lee," Mr. Darby said, "the wall is in his way. Help him out, please."

Lee-Lee unzipped a pocket on her cargo pants, and chameleons began to climb out, one after another. They streamed down her leg, crawled across the floor, and then clambered up the wall, their tiny claws puncturing the plaster. Dozens crawled through the open doorway to get to the other side of the wall. Then, as they spread out, the wall seemed to slowly disappear. But Noah knew what was really happening. The chameleons were blending the wall into the surroundings, which, from Noah's perspective, happened to be the kitchen and the people in it. In a matter of seconds, the wall between the kitchen and the living room appeared to be gone.

"Better?" Mr. Darby asked.

Noah nodded. Six Descenders were guarding the portal to the City of Species. Dozens of tarsiers, who'd followed the Descenders into Noah's house, oftentimes clinging to their clothes, were perched along the kitchen furniture, countertop, and cabinets, surveying the scene with their big, bulging eyes. The curtain was still blowing in the wind from the City of Species, revealing glimpses of the dark streets.

Megan was standing off to one side, wiping tears from her cheeks with the back of her hand while Elakshi tried to console her. She'd just shared the story of her escape from DeGraff. Podgy had flown in from the treetops, knocked over the security guard who was holding her captive, and flown off again, this time with Megan clinging to his back. He'd headed straight for the portal to Megan's kitchen.

"My parents," Noah said as he stared at the portal. "This is my fault."

"Noah," Mr. Darby said, "you can't—"

"I can!" Noah said, suddenly angry. "I've known what's been going on—for more than a *year*! And I never warned them!"

"At my request," Mr. Darby said. "If anyone should harbor the blame, then let it be me. *I* endangered your parents, Noah. Not you."

Noah shook his head. In truth, it didn't matter whose fault it was. All that mattered was that his parents were gone, captured by a lunatic and taken to another world that was

140

quickly falling to darkness.

Noah checked the clock: 10:37. Then he said, "Charlie told me that DeGraff is planning to attack at midnight tonight. They're coming for my world."

Mr. Darby became quiet. He glanced at Solana, Sam, Hannah. "Then I'm glad we're already taking action."

Just as Noah was about to ask what Mr. Darby meant, Zak walked down the stairs—he'd come from the portal in Noah's closet. The Teknikal had a big, full sack slung over his shoulder, reminding Noah of a bizarre Santa Claus—one with a Mohawk, dirty overalls, and a tank top.

Zak winked as he stepped into the room and dropped the sack, startling Blizzard. "Here you go, Mr. D."

Mr. Darby looked down at the sack and combed his fingers through his beard. "They're ready?"

"As ready as they'll ever be."

"And the Primary Portal?"

"Almost. My Teks are working nonstop."

"Almost isn't good enough," Mr. Darby said. He nodded toward the portal in the kitchen. "It has to be now."

Noah said, "I don't...what are you guys *talking* about?"

Zak reached into the sack and pulled out a disk the size of his palm. "This. A Magic Modifier. We call them mods."

Noah glanced at Solana, and it was obvious that she didn't understand, either.

"Tell them," Mr. Darby said.

Zak held up the mod. "They recalibrate the magic in the curtains. All you have to do is press this button"—he showed them the button, but didn't touch it—"and a signal goes out, transforming the magic in any gateway within a quarter mile. Those gateways will then open to wherever the Primary Portal is placed."

Noah stared at the mod and remembered the example Mr. Darby had shown him with the knickknacks—three pieces of velvet magically connected to a single point.

"The Multipoint," Noah said.

Mr. Darby nodded. "Think of a bunch of doors that open to a single room. All we have to do is place the mods and activate the Primary Portal."

"Are you sure it will work?" Noah asked.

Zak nodded. Then he shrugged. Then he nodded again.

"It's never been performed on a large scale, Noah," Mr. Darby explained. "Just tested in our labs—what I showed you with the knickknacks." He turned to Zak and added, "We need to place them as soon as possible. Noah learned that DeGraff is sending his army at midnight."

"Midnight?"

Mr. Darby nodded.

Zak's stare went blank as he considered something for a moment. Then he said, "The mods are ready, but like I said, my Teks are still finishing up the Primary Portal."

"Then tell them to hurry." Mr. Darby glanced around

142

the room, adding, "I'll need volunteers to place the mods. We need one in every exhibit at the Clarksville Zoo. And we need them scattered throughout the neighborhood to take care of any new portals that DeGraff may have created, like the one in the school. Keep them away from Noah's house." He pointed to the curtain in the kitchen. "We need that portal to continue working like it is. Same for the portal in Noah's closet."

Sara, one of the Specters, raised her hand. "I think we're the obvious choice," she said. "The Specters can get across the neighborhood and the Clarksville Zoo undetected."

"Agreed," Mr. Darby said. "You'll have to be fast."

"I can help," Solana said.

"No," Sara quickly spoke up. "We can do this alone."

Solana jumped to her feet. "Mr. Darby, we have a little more than an hour before—"

"I said *no*."

"Sara, you're not—"

Mr. Darby waved a hand out in front of him, as if batting their argument out of the air. "Enough! Now isn't the time to continue this squabble!"

Noah glanced at Sara and Solana. He'd seen the tension between the Specters and Descenders for a long time, but he didn't understand it. He was tired of not knowing.

"What's going on between you?" he asked.

Sara, still staring at Solana, tipped her head Noah's way and said, "Tell him."

Solana started to say something but then stopped. She looked at Noah out of the corner of her eye.

"Tell me," Noah said. "I want to know."

Solana shook her head, and for a few seconds, Noah was sure she'd stay quiet. But then she gazed at the floor by her feet and started talking.

"Years ago, a few Specters found out that some Descenders were using their powers to rob homes just outside the City of Species. When the Descenders learned that the Specters were going to turn them in, they captured all the Specters they could, dragged them into the Grottoes, and pushed them through a portal that they knew went amiss. Evie, Sara, Lee-Lee...the six Specters you've met...they were the only ones to escape."

Solana became quiet and continued to stare at the floor, clearly ashamed. Sara stood with hers arms crossed and her eyes full of accusation.

Noah, knowing that people who "went amiss" basically disappeared, asked the question that seemed most critical: "Did you go after them?"

"Pointless," Mr. Darby said. "It was a faulty portal, and no one ever returned from it. The portal was ordered to be taken down. We can only hope that the lost Specters are safe—able to pick up their lives in whatever place they're

144

in."

Sara suddenly turned to Mr. Darby and said, "Send us—me and the girls! We'll find them!" Noah could tell by her sharp tone that this wasn't the first time she and Mr. Darby had had this conversation.

"It's not safe. It wouldn't—"

"And what *is* safe?" Sara glanced around the room. "*This?* I've been doing unsafe things for as long as I can remember!"

Mr. Darby stayed quiet for a long time. Then he frowned and said, "Sara, it might be time to let them go. In your heart."

"They were my *friends*!" Sara said, her voice breaking with emotion. "My family!"

"I know," Mr. Darby said. "And I'm sorry. But the portal is closed. The curtain…it's gone."

"So let's put it back up!" Sara glanced at Zak and added, "He can recalibrate it!"

"Perhaps," Mr. Darby said. "But the risk of more life…"

"I'm not concerned about that!"

"I know, but I am. I have to be. If I weren't, I wouldn't be fit to lead the Secret Zoo."

Sara started to say something more but stopped. She glanced between Solana and Mr. Darby, and then took a step back, her arms still crossed.

"And now," Mr. Darby continued, "in the way of leadership, I'm ordering you to take Solana with you into the Clarksville Zoo."

Sara rolled her eyes but stayed quiet. After a few seconds, the Specters began to gather—Sara, Lee-Lee, Elakshi, Jordynn, Kaleena—all except for Evie, who was still with Ella. They began to fill the normal pockets on their cargo pants with the mods.

As Noah watched the Specters prepare, he thought of everything that had happened that night. He thought of his parents and the way their bedroom had looked. He remembered being dragged across the floor. Then he recalled how the firefly light had affected Charlie.

Noah said, "With all that light—Charlie changed."

Mr. Darby turned to Noah, one eyebrow raised. "How so?"

"His arms—they weren't so freakishly long anymore. And his freckles looked normal."

Everyone was now listening. Even the Descenders in the other room were staring at Noah through the wall that appeared to be invisible.

"But Charlie walks around in the light all the time," Mr. Darby said. "The sasquatches, too."

"Yeah, but not DeGraff—he also got hit by the light."

Mr. Darby held his gaze on Noah. "What are you trying to say?"

146

Noah looked around the room—the Specters, the Descenders, his sister. "All the animals and people are like DeGraff's prisoners. Would bringing down DeGraff free them?"

"Council has raised this question before," Mr. Darby said. "We've never seen evidence to suggest this would work. We—"

"I saw evidence," Noah said. "Tonight. Charlie changed—I saw that."

Mr. Darby considered this some more. After a few seconds, he said, "Charlie already has a wicked heart. He—"

"Yeah, Charlie does. But not the others. Even the sasquatches—they're unruly, but they're not evil."

Mr. Darby glanced at Zak, as if to see what he was thinking. Then he looked at Lee-Lee, Solana, Sam.

"Tonight wasn't the first time I saw how light hurts DeGraff," Noah added. "I saw it in the Secret Chamber of Lights. The flashlight fish—they started shining all at once, and DeGraff dropped to his knees." Noah looked at his sister and said, "Remember?"

Megan nodded.

"What if we filled the Secret Zoo with light—so much light that DeGraff couldn't escape into the shadows again?"

"And how do we do that, bro?" Zak asked. He motioned to the gateway and the stormy streets behind it.

Noah shrugged. "Do you have something, Zak? Some

kind of device that can shine light everywhere?"

Zak shook his head.

Noah turned and faced the curtain, which was still blowing in the wind. He looked into the dark, foggy streets of the City of Species. Shadowy animals were stalking around, and it chilled him to know that they could see him. He saw the silhouettes of buildings and tall trees, and a winding loop of the glass waterslide that descended from the Wotter Tower. Across the street stood a small, familiar shop. Noah squinted for a closer look and realized it was Lots of Latte, the coffee shop where, a few days ago, Mr. Darby had given the Specters instructions for rescuing Tank and the Descenders.

He stood, wincing at the pain in his hand when he used it for support, and slowly walked across the living room, his gaze fixed on the coffee shop and a sudden flurry of ideas in his head. He noticed the wall between the kitchen and the living room—or the *absence* of the wall, really. The chameleons, their magic.

"I have an idea," he said.

Everyone stood still and listened.

CHAPTER 16

THE BLIZZARD BEFORE THE STORM

"Do you know the quickest way from the Institute of Light?" Mr. Darby asked.

Lee-Lee adjusted a buckle on her boot and said, "Through the alleys and across Arctic Town."

"Go fast, Lee-Lee. And remember to wait for the signal from the other Specters."

Lee-Lee nodded. Then she turned and pushed through the portal in Noah's closet. Noah and Mr. Darby watched the curtain settle. Then they walked back into Noah's bedroom.

"The first step in your plan has been executed, Noah. Let's hope it goes well."

The floorboards began to groan and shift beneath Noah's feet. He turned and saw Blizzard walking into his room. The polar bear made his way to him and partly leaned against his leg.

Mr. Darby reached into his jacket, pulled out a gold pocket watch, and checked it. "It will take some time for Solana and the Specters to place the mods. You should try to rest."

"Rest? How?"

"Just close your eyes and breathe deeply." Mr. Darby headed for the door, adding, "I'll radio Ella and Richie and have them come at once."

As the old man walked out of his room, Noah heard the muffled sounds of the people downstairs: nervous chatter, and Zak's shrill voice. In his room, Blizzard softly growled and stared up at Noah, his beady black eyes looking like shiny pebbles. Noah forced a smile and stroked the bear's fur, taking comfort in the motions.

"Bliz, I'm scared."

The polar bear looked at Noah in a way that showed he understood.

Noah walked to his window. He glanced toward Fort Scout and thought about everything that had brought him to this point. He remembered the clues that had led him to the Secret Zoo—the flyer that Marlo had dropped in his room, and the pages from Megan's diary that the animals had secretly delivered. He thought of walking through the Library of the Secret Society, and of his time in Metr-APE-olis, swinging from the hands of apes like a circus performer on a trapeze. He remembered learning the truth about the Descenders: Sam and his feathery wings; Tameron and his powerful tail; Hannah and her magical boots; Solana and her quills.

Solana. In Noah's thoughts, she jumped forward. Noah saw her long dark hair, her soft skin. He remembered the time in the Forest of Flight when they'd sat so close on a bench—the way the side of her leg had felt pressed against his. Then he remembered how Ella had approached him later, her arms crossed and her face full of disapproval. *She's too old for you,* she'd said. *And she has quills...like a porcupine.*

Noah smiled and thought about his friends. Ella, a sarcastic tomboy with an all-pink wardrobe. Richie, a proud nerd with books stored in his brain. Megan, his sister, a girl he'd shared a lifetime with.

He looked out at his neighborhood, the only world he'd known until discovering the Secret Zoo. He imagined DeGraff's animals storming down his street, sasquatches breaking down doors and attacking. How many lives were at risk? People Noah knew and loved.

He listened again to the sounds downstairs: Mr. Darby's muffled voice, the rumble of footsteps. The Secret Society was planning, preparing. Noah's idea would work—it would work because it had to.

He felt a sudden, sharp pain in his palm and glanced at his hand. The towel was partly covered in blood, and he could still feel the burn from the firefly.

Something thumped against his bedroom floor, and Noah jumped. He was relieved to see Blizzard stretched out, his soft belly pressed to the carpet. Noah, realizing how tired he was, lay down and leaned against the polar bear.

Remembering what Mr. Darby had said about resting, Noah nestled into a more comfortable spot, making a pillow in Blizzard's furry side. Within seconds, his eyes started to close. Instead of fighting it, he took a deep breath and accepted what his body needed to do.

*

"Wait!" Ella said as she stepped out onto her front porch.

"What's wrong?" Evie whispered. The two had just talked to Mr. Darby and were now on their way to Noah's house, their bodies camouflaged by the chameleons.

"I have to do something," Ella said, and she made her way back inside.

"Do what?" Evie called out.

But Ella was already halfway up the stairs, stepping in the spots that didn't creak. She walked into her mother's room, tiptoed across the floor, and then stood beside the bed.

Her mother was sleeping a deep sleep, the kind Ella hadn't known for a while, not since becoming a Crosser and beginning her double life, lying to the people she loved.

Memories of times spent with her mother played in Ella's head. Going for ice cream after soccer games. Matinee movies on rainy days. Long talks at night while her mother sat on the edge of Ella's bed. Her mother. The woman who had fed her, clothed her. The woman who had taught her what it meant to be loved.

A cool draft moved through the room, and as Ella's mother rolled over in her sleep, her blanket slipped off her arm. Ella waited and watched. When her mother didn't stir again, Ella grabbed the blanket and gently pulled it up. Then she leaned across the bed. And because she couldn't risk waking her mother by kissing her cheek, she gently kissed her shoulder instead.

I love you, Mom, she mouthed.

She stood up straight and felt the sadness in her smile. Then she turned and fled the room, worried she'd never see the person she loved most in this world again.

*

Richie paused at his parents' room and stared through the doorway. His mom and dad were fast asleep.

Tank grabbed Richie's arm and whispered, "C'mon."

Richie nodded, forgetting that Tank couldn't see him because they'd camouflaged themselves in order to sneak out of the house. Then he turned his attention back to his parents. It seemed crazy that he'd been able to sneak around, in and out of two worlds, for more than a year without his parents knowing. And it felt deceitful. A part of him wanted to wake his mom and dad and tell them everything. It would be nice to be honest for a change. But Richie knew he couldn't. As incredible as it still seemed, Richie, a boy from the small city of Clarksville, had two worlds to save.

"Guys..." Richie whispered, "I love you."

He waited, partly hoping his mother or father might wake up and see him—stop him from doing what he now needed to do. But they didn't, and after a few seconds, Tank squeezed his arm and gently pulled him down the hall.

The two walked down the stairs and into the living room. As they headed for the front door, Richie saw the couch and thought of all the times his family had gathered to talk, laugh, and worry when things weren't going right. Richie would sometimes cuddle up to them, even in recent years.

His gaze wandered to other things in the room. The family pictures that never seemed to hang straight. The brown stains on the carpet from Richie's muddy shoes. The ugly lamp that shined too bright. Things made perfect by their imperfections. Little pieces of a bigger puzzle—a place called home. Richie worried it would go away if he walked out the door.

"Richie," Tank said, "we have to go."

Richie turned his attention to the front door, which was partly open.

"Little man," Tank said, "we need you."

Richie thought about how much he meant to his parents. Then he stepped onto the porch and gently closed the door behind him. As he and Tank walked across his front yard, Richie's head filled with memories of his family. And as they headed down the street, Richie found himself

154

repeatedly glancing back. His house grew smaller and smaller. And before long, it faded into darkness, just like Richie feared it would.

CHAPTER 17

ITY T EA S ND SE T R WE S

As Lee-Lee, still in camouflage, approached the small building that had once been a bakery in the Streets of Transparency, she looked up at the storefront sign: ITY T EA S ND SE T R WE S. A few of the letters that spelled *City Treats and Sector Sweets* appeared to be missing because chameleons were camouflaging them as they crawled over the sign and the rest of the store. The Specter made her way onto the porch, carefully tiptoeing into open spots between the chameleons and hoping not to step on any that weren't visible. Then she moved through the door and across the old bakery, where hundreds of chameleons covered the counter, the ovens, and the registers, and filled the glass cabinets that had held baked goods many years ago.

She quickly made her way to the small room in the back of the store. As she stood just inside the doorway, she surveyed the space: forty-eight canvas sacks hanging from steel storage racks, and hundreds of chameleons crawling around. Once used to hold flour, the sacks were now magically connected to the pockets in the Specters' pants.

Lee-Lee fixed her gaze on the sacks. She waited, knowing the signal from Jordynn should be coming soon, and wondering if Noah's outlandish plan to save her world could possibly work.

CHAPTER 18

11:34

"Noah, wake up."

Noah opened one eye and realized he was lying on his back, his head resting against the furry mound of Blizzard's side. Someone was standing over him. Sam.

"You better get ready," Sam said.

Noah pushed himself up to a seated position and almost screamed at the sudden pain in his hand. He saw the bloody hand towel and remembered what had happened in the kitchen. He quickly got to his feet.

"Here," Sam said. He handed over Tameron's backpack and walked out of the bedroom.

Noah slipped his arms through the straps and felt the now familiar weight of the pack. Blizzard quickly got up. Marlo sprang off the windowsill and took up his usual perch on Noah's shoulder.

"You ready, Bliz?"

The big bear fixed his dark eyes on Noah and grunted.

Noah spotted his watch on the nearby desk and put it on, thinking he might need it. As he headed out of his bedroom, Blizzard followed closely, his weight bending the boards beneath their feet. Noah walked down four or five steps and suddenly stopped when his view opened to the scene on the first floor. Tarsiers were clinging to kitchen cabinets and dangling from appliances. Podgy was waddling around, his flippers softly wagging. And P-Dog and the other prairie dogs were sniffing scents out of the carpet. The wall between the kitchen and living room still appeared to be missing—the work of the chameleons.

Noah turned his attention to a familiar voice and saw Tank. The big man was leaning against one wall, his arms crossed and his muscles bulging. Noah headed toward the living room, Blizzard following, and saw the other scouts. At a time when everything was changing at a dizzying rate, they were the one constant, and Noah was thankful for it.

Ella walked up to him, grabbed his wrist, and looked at the bloody towel on his hand.

"It's okay," Noah said. "Has anyone told you our plan?"

Ella nodded. "Mr. Darby."

"Where's Evie?"

"She left. She's helping the other Specters place the mods."

"Except for Lee-Lee and Jordynn," Noah corrected, knowing the two Specters were part of his plan.

He looked toward the portal and saw the group of Descenders guarding it. The curtain was blowing in the wind, allowing the sounds and smells of the City of Species to continue to invade the house. Noah saw glimpses of silhouettes and the red eyes of the animals—pairs of glowing dots floating in the dim light. Inside the Secret Zoo, groups of animals appeared to be moving in specific directions.

"Mr. Darby?" Noah said, and the name came out like a question.

Mr. Darby, who wasn't standing far from the scouts, looked at Noah. "Yes?"

"Something...something's happening."

When Mr. Darby saw what Noah did, he quickly made his way into the kitchen. The scouts followed, stepping over the prairie dogs in their path. At the portal, the old man pulled back the entire curtain. The animals were flooding into the various sectors, and it was obvious where they were headed. The Clarksville Zoo.

Blizzard squeezed into a spot between Noah and Richie. Tank and other Descenders loomed behind the scouts. Even the tarsiers were watching from their places on the kitchen cabinets.

Mr. Darby checked his pocket watch and said, "Eleven thirty-seven." He looked back at the red-eyed animals walking across the streets and streams. "It's happening." He touched the transmit button on his headset and said, "Evie— DeGraff is staging his army. What's the status on the mods?"

"We have more than half in place."

160

"Then move faster. Midnight's almost here."

"We already—"

"Move faster, Evie! Find a way!" Mr. Darby turned to Tank and said, "You're in charge now."

Noah saw something on Tank's face that he almost never did. Worry.

"Mr. D," Tank said, "what are you going to do?"

"What Noah planned for us to do. It starts with distracting DeGraff."

The creator of the Secret Zoo frowned. He glanced at Noah, Megan, Sam. Then he marched through the portal and into the City of Species.

CHAPTER 19

11:38

Noah just stood there, unsure what to think. He stared straight ahead and caught glimpses of Mr. Darby, the end of his long jacket sweeping along the wet streets. When the old man cupped his hands to his mouth and hollered "DeGraff!" his voice crossed the threshold between the two worlds and echoed in Noah's kitchen. A few startled tarsiers jumped down from the cabinets, and prairie dogs scattered.

"Sam," Tank said, "I'll radio Zak when we get inside. As soon as he's ready, I need you to go to Teknikal Tower and get the Primary Portal. Zak will be on the twenty-third floor. Fly by the window, and I'll have Zak toss the curtain to you. The mod, too. Get straight to Koala Kastle and hang it in the courtyard."

Sam nodded.

"Be quick about it," the big man added. He glanced out at the city—at Mr. Darby crossing the streets and at the groups of monstrous animals, which didn't seem interested in Mr. Darby as they headed into the various sectors.

Mr. Darby's voice echoed in the kitchen as he called out for DeGraff once more. Noah caught another glimpse of the old man, the leader of a hidden world where penguins can fly and animals share the streets with people.

"Everyone know the plan?" Tank asked as he glanced at Noah to signify whose plan it was.

The Crossers nodded and exchanged worried looks. Noah adjusted his backpack.

"Good," Tank said. "Then let's go."

The big man turned and walked through the portal. And everyone followed.

CHAPTER 20

11:39

The Crossers gathered just beyond the portal and watched Mr. Darby walk deeper into the Secret Zoo. Dark storm clouds loomed overhead, leaving everything in silhouette and shadow. The monstrous animals were flooding into the sectors, and the tall trees shook as thousands of sick birds jumped from branch to branch. The once colorful leaves were now wilted and weak. It chilled Noah to think that the City of Species might soon look as desolate and dead as the Dark Lands, the sector the sasquatches had once occupied. He could feel DeGraff's magic in the air—he could feel it in his heart and mind, an actual weight that would eventually crush the goodness in Noah, given enough time.

"We need to guard this portal," Tank said, gesturing to the one that opened to Noah's kitchen. He motioned to the Descenders and said, "Make sure nothing gets through."

A group of Descenders spread out along the wide curtain, their animal powers ready to strike. Blizzard moved into position as well.

"Zak—you ready?"

Noah realized Tank was talking into his radio.

"Now?" Noah was able to hear Zak in his headset—his voice and his surprise. "No! I need at least ten minutes!"

"You got five," Tank said. "Look out the window."

The airwaves went silent. Then Zak said, "What's Darby doing?"

"He's going after DeGraff. This is happening now."

A few seconds passed without a response. Then Zak said, "Okay, five minutes."

"I'll send Sam to your window," Tank said. "It's the quickest way."

"Roger," Zak said. And then the airwaves stayed silent.

Tank turned to Jordynn, the only Specter still with the group, and the scouts. "Get into camo, and somebody ghost me."

As the scouts opened their pockets and allowed the chameleons to crawl out onto them, Jordynn walked over to Tank and shared some of her chameleons with him. Their bodies started to blur, and then seemed to disappear altogether. On Noah's shoulder, Marlo also blended into the surroundings.

"Head for the coffee shop," Tank said.

Lots of Latte was about a hundred yards away. As Noah headed in that direction, he kept his attention on Mr. Darby. The old man raised his arms and shouted, "I'm here, old friend!"

Friend. Never had the term been more untrue. DeGraff and Mr. Darby wanted each other dead—they'd wanted it for *more* than a lifetime.

A long fountain in the middle of the street had a waist-high wall. Mr. Darby climbed onto it and began to walk along the ledge, his arms out to his sides and his voice louder than ever: "I'm here, DeGraff! Why do you hide?" The animals plowing into the sectors continued to ignore him.

Noah suddenly remembered his parents and said, "Megan—did you see where they took Mom and Dad?"

"No. All the noise and animals—and it was so dark!"

Mr. Darby continued to call out his rival's name. He turned a slow circle on the ledge of the fountain and hollered, "Let's end this!"

Just then, a figure jumped up from the water and grabbed Mr. Darby's legs. DeGraff. He pulled the old man into the fountain, splashing water everywhere. Then he pounced on his victim, and both men disappeared behind the short wall.

"Mr. Darby!" Ella screamed.

"Quiet!" Tank said. "This is what he wants."

"To *die*?" Ella asked.

Tank shook his head. "To battle."

Mr. Darby appeared in the waist-high water about fifty feet away from DeGraff. Noah had no idea how he'd managed to slip away from the Shadowist. DeGraff looked down at himself and peeled a wet leaf off his jacket. Then he straightened his fedora and smiled, the old wounds on his face spreading in a grotesque way. "Clever," he said.

"You can't do this," Mr. Darby said.

DeGraff laughed, and it was a sickening sound—noise bubbling up from his chest. "Stand proud, old man. Let's not end this in clichés."

"You mistake me," Mr. Darby said. "I mean you *can't* do this. I won't let you."

DeGraff laughed harder this time. "Look around, fool! You've already lost."

"Have I?" Mr. Darby said. He raised his arms out to his sides again and added, "I'm still standing."

"Yes," DeGraff said. "But not for long."

The Shadowist disappeared, leaving ripples in the water where he'd stood. He immediately jumped up behind Mr. Darby, but as he attacked, Mr. Darby leaned over, and Noah witnessed a new impossible: Mr. Darby's jacket changed form. It rounded outward, and the fabric became hard and smooth, a shiny surface with a pattern of connected shapes. A shell. DeGraff tried to grab on to the surface, but couldn't, and Mr. Darby swung around, easily slipping out of his grasp. Then he stood up straight and the shell changed back into his normal jacket.

Out of the corner of his eye, Noah noticed movement back at the portal to his kitchen. Sam and the other

Descenders were kneeling in the street, bowing their heads like knights before a king, just as they had outside Creepy Critters after DeGraff had escaped.

"Tank!" Noah said. "What…what are they doing?"

"Reverence," Tank explained. "Reverence for the first Descender."

"What?"

Tank simply gave time for his words to sink in.

Noah turned his attention back to the battle in the fountain. DeGraff struggled to find his balance. Then he reached into his jacket and withdrew a long knife. "Looks like you want to make this interesting."

The Shadowist charged, his arm pulled back and his knife readied. But as he delivered what should have been a deadly blow, Mr. Darby fell to his knees, and his open jacket draped over his sides. Twelve-inch barbs sprang out from the velvet, just like they did on Solana's clothes, and DeGraff fell on top of him. The Shadowist cried out in pain and then rolled off into the water. When he stood again, Noah saw barbs sticking out from his thighs. DeGraff ripped them from his flesh—or what remained of his flesh, anyway.

As incredible as it seemed, Mr. Darby had more than one animal power.

DeGraff attacked again, and Mr. Darby sprang high into the air, like Hannah, and landed behind his assailant.

A voice rose over the airwaves: "Ready when you are."

Zak. He had the Primary Portal configured.

"Got it," Tank said. "Don't forget to hand off the mod that activates the portal."

Noah looked back at Sam, who'd gotten the message as well. Sam raised his arms over his head and brought them back down, striking the zippers on his wrists against the buckles on his hips. Then he lifted his arms again, releasing his feathery wings. He squatted and jumped into the sky. Noah watched him soar, veering around trees and the glass tubes of the Wotter Slide as he made his way to Teknikal Tower.

As Tank and the scouts closed to within fifty yards of the coffee shop, Mr. Darby turned and his jacket became the shell again. This time, he kicked out with his powerful legs and plowed into DeGraff. As the two slid across the fountain, spilling water over the sides, DeGraff escaped into the shadows and appeared in a new spot, water dripping off the brim of his fedora.

Noah turned to look toward Teknikal Tower just as Sam was attacked by a group of orangutans in a nearby tree. One of Sam's wings bent, and the Descender began to spiral toward the ground. He hit the street and rolled, his grunts booming across the airwaves.

"Sam!" Tank said. "Sam—you okay?"

Silence over the airwaves. On the streets beneath the orangutans, the fallen Descender didn't move.

169

"Sam!"

More silence, and then finally, Sam's voice, wounded and weak: "I'm...I'm all right." Sam staggered to his feet and glanced around. "The Primary Portal! I dropped it!"

"It's in the tree!" Ella said.

Noah saw the curtain hanging over a branch high above Sam. More than a dozen orangutans were swinging across the tree to get to it. Sam tried to fly and couldn't.

"Podgy!" Noah cried out.

Back at the portal to Noah's kitchen, Podgy took several strides and then leaped into the air. Noah opened his right pocket to come out of his camouflage, hoping DeGraff wouldn't notice. On his shoulder, Marlo appeared as well. Podgy spotted Noah and flew his way. Seconds later, he touched down near the scout, his webbed feet clapping against the street. Then he turned his back to Noah, just like he had in the Dark Lands and the window box outside Noah's room.

"Go!" Tank said to Noah. "We can do our part without you!"

Noah worried about the extra weight of his backpack. He considered taking it off but decided against it. Then he walked closer to Podgy, saying, "Fly above the curtain. I'll grab it as you pass."

Podgy wagged his flippers to show that he understood. He started to run, and as Noah charged behind him, Marlo

170

jumped off his shoulder and flew alongside. When Podgy jumped into the air, Noah wrapped his arms around the penguin's blubbery midsection. The two veered to one side and Noah felt certain they'd crash. But Podgy gained control and the winged duo soared up and up. It took only a few seconds for Podgy to close in on the Primary Portal.

"Get as close as you can!" Noah said.

He glanced over and saw Marlo—the tiny kingfisher was still flying beside them, a blue blur in front of the dark skies.

As they closed in on the Primary Portal, so did the orangutans, leaping from branch to branch. Podgy veered to avoid them. One orangutan jumped at Noah and just missed grabbing his ankle. Another leaped at Podgy, who dipped out of the way at the last second. As Podgy flew over the curtain, Noah reached out and snatched it. Then Podgy weaved through the limbs and punched out on the other side of the tree.

"I got it!" Noah said into his headset.

Sam's voice rose over the airwaves. "The mod—you need the mod!"

Noah looked down and saw Sam waving the mod above his head. Podgy dipped low to the ground, and as the duo passed over Sam, the Descender tossed up the device. Noah reached out with one hand, got his arm wrapped in the curtain, and nearly missed the catch. But his fingers closed

171

on the mod, and he was able to stuff it into his jacket pocket.

"Koala Kastle!" Noah said. "Podge—get us there!"

As Podgy swerved down a dark alley, Noah's legs swung out and he nearly slipped off the penguin's back, narrowly avoiding being thrown against the wall. Both sides of the alley reached up and out of sight—brick walls covered in green ivy. Frogs and birds and other small creatures looked out from the leaves, their eyes glowing red. Podgy veered around branches and steel balconies. Then he flew out onto a new street. As he headed for the open front doors to the Forest of Flight, Noah realized that cutting through the sector would provide a shortcut to Koala Kastle.

Inside the Forest of Flight, birds crowded the heights. They hadn't been affected by DeGraff's dark magic because the building had protected them from the storm. Hundreds of hummingbirds flew around, streaking bright colors across the landscape. When the tiny birds saw Podgy and Marlo, they chased after them, almost in a playful way, soaring beside waterfalls and wet, rocky cliffs. At the other side of the sector, Podgy flew through an open window and Noah's toes skipped off the frame.

As Koala Kastle came into view, Podgy veered toward the entrance, a velvet curtain hanging in front of an opening in the wall. Into his headset, Noah said, "We're inbound—closing in on Koala Kastle."

Tank's voice came through the airwaves:

"Remember—you're going into a sector, not an ordinary building. You'll lose communications when you cross."

"Roger," Noah said as Podgy neared the curtain—twenty feet, fifteen feet, ten. "Good luck, Tank."

"Same to you, kid. Just hang the Primary Portal and get—"

Tank's voice stopped as the curtain swept off Noah's back and he and Podgy entered the sector.

The first thing Noah saw was Koala Kastle, a sprawling, storybook castle built on the rocky top of a mountain. The second thing he saw was a sasquatch, an upright creature with bulging muscles and scraggly hair. The beast swung its arm and connected with Podgy. As the emperor penguin was thrown to the side, he tipped, and Noah slipped down his back, his legs banging and dragging across a drawbridge. Then Noah lost his grip and crashed to the wooden planks.

Noah lay there, his head spinning. After a few seconds, he staggered to his feet and looked around. He was on a long drawbridge that crossed a ravine that looked like something from the Grand Canyon. Hundreds of feet below, a river raged. The drawbridge was easily half the length of a football field. The thick wooden planks connected an expansive mountain wall to the mountaintop Koala Kastle was built upon.

Sasquatches stood on both sides of Noah, two in front

173

and three in back, their mangy fur dangling from their outstretched arms, their gazes fixed on him.

"Podgy!" Noah called out. He looked left, then right, and then spotted Marlo and Podgy flying circles off to one side of the drawbridge.

He realized he'd dropped the Primary Portal. He saw it lying on the bridge and quickly picked it up. He thought of the mod and checked his jacket pocket. Still there. Then he looked toward Koala Kastle and saw the open courtyard he needed to get to. It was about a hundred feet past the end of the drawbridge.

Noah heard a long, slow growl. A sasquatch was standing close by, its eyes glowing red and bloody drool dangling from its chapped lips. The beast lunged at Noah, who threw himself to one side at the last second and then took off running. The other sasquatches attacked, their arms swinging and their razor-sharp claws slicing through the air. Noah ducked and dodged, barely missing the blows. He dove between the legs of a sasquatch, rolled once on the bridge, and came to his feet running.

His heart raced as his heels pounded the boards. He ran thirty feet, forty feet. Then he abruptly stopped near the middle of the drawbridge as a new pack of sasquatches stepped off the mountaintop and onto the wooden planks. He glanced back and forth. The sasquatches had both ends of the drawbridge blocked. They started charging toward him, and

Noah could feel their weighty footfalls in the boards beneath his feet. He was trapped—the sasquatches would reach him in seconds.

"*Podgy!*" Noah called out, his arms waving above his head.

Less than fifty feet away, the penguin veered toward Noah. Noah could tell he was planning to sweep low over the drawbridge so Noah could grab on. It wouldn't be easy—Noah had the curtain to consider, and he also had the added weight of the backpack.

His thoughts stopped. The backpack. Maybe he could plow through the sasquatches and get to the mountaintop. He grabbed the drawstrings on his shoulder straps. Two pulls and he would be ready to fight.

The sasquatches slowed down and nervously glanced at one another. They'd battled enough Descenders to understand what Noah was planning.

Pull the cords, a voice inside Noah said. *Pull the cords and fight!*

He thought of Sam and Hannah and Solana, the way they handled things, with force. But grabbing onto Podgy seemed the better choice. Surely he could hold on long enough for the penguin to fly him to safety.

Podgy was less than twenty feet away and closing fast. To free his hands, Noah draped the curtain across his shoulders. Then he prepared to jump. The sasquatches

175

charged again, causing the planks to quake.

As Podgy flew over the drawbridge, Noah jumped onto the penguin's back. His toes dragged along the boards, and then his feet felt the open air. Podgy was over the river—and so was Noah.

He told himself not to look down, but the urge was irresistible. The mountain walls looked like steep cliffs with a few trees growing from flat patches of land. The distant river looked like a trickle of water.

As Podgy veered toward the safety of the mountaintop, Noah felt his hold slip. When he tried to grab back on, the wind pulled the Primary Portal out from under him. Noah instinctively reached for it, came off Podgy's back, and began to freefall into the ravine, his clothes fluttering and snapping, his organs floating in his body. Above him, Podgy, his only hope for rescue, grew smaller and smaller and quickly became nothing more than a black dot—a distant bird in the sky.

Chapter 21

11:43

"How does it look?" Jordynn asked.

Silence. Ella looked around and wondered if Jordynn was talking to her. She couldn't tell because she couldn't see her—or Richie or Megan or Tank. The five of them were still camouflaged.

"Perfect," said a deep voice. Tank.

"It's crazy," Richie said, and Ella realized he was standing right beside her. "It's like…it's like it's not even there."

Ella thought the same thing. They could see out all around them into the City of Species, where DeGraff and Mr. Darby were still fighting in the streets.

"Mirage complete," Jordynn said into her headset. "Sending signal."

Ella looked in the direction she thought Jordynn was and saw something appear—a figurine, a small porcelain clown with an oversized nose. A second later, the clown was gone. Jordynn had dropped the knickknack from Noah's house—the signal—into a pocket that opened to the old bakery in the Streets of Transparency, the place where the Specters' chameleons were kept, and the place where Lee-Lee was waiting.

Ella held her breath, hoping Lee-Lee would get the message—and wondering what would happen next.

CHAPTER 22

11:44

Tink.

Lee-Lee barely heard the sound. She scanned the chameleon-covered floor for the clown figurine—the signal. She gazed left, right. Nothing. Just hundreds of chameleons crawling on and off one another. Every so often, she'd catch a glimpse of the floor.

She saw a small flash of white and locked her stare. She waited. She watched. Then she saw a second flash of white. The chameleons were crawling on and off an object—the porcelain clown.

Lee-Lee took a deep breath. Jordynn and the scouts were ready.

She moved into the room, using her feet to gently sweep chameleons out of her way. At the first storage rack, she took down a canvas sack and shook it in the air like a sandy beach towel to get the chameleons off. She folded the sack, set it on the rack, and went to work on a second sack, flinging chameleons around. Then she went to the third sack, the fourth, the fifth. When she was finished with the last one, she tucked them under her arm, left the room, and quickly exited the old bakery.

On the Streets of Transparency, she touched the transmit button on her headset and said, "I'm on my way," to anyone who might be able to hear. Then she ran down the street toward her new destination.

.

CHAPTER 23

11:45

DeGraff plowed into Mr. Darby, and the two splashed into the water. A gloved hand pushed down on Mr. Darby's head, and the side of his face pressed against the concrete bottom of the fountain. He grabbed his jacket near the front collar and held it over his face like a mask. Then he took a deep breath and drew in the water, which passed through the filter of the fabric, allowing only oxygen into his lungs. The velvet acted like gills, allowing him to breathe underwater— another animal power.

He waited for time to pass—one minute, and then two. He stopped struggling and became perfectly still, pretending to be dead. DeGraff, convinced that his wicked work was done, slowly stood. Mr. Darby, still breathing oxygen through his jacket, waited. After a few seconds, the water around him stirred, and he realized DeGraff was walking off. He jumped up, pounced on DeGraff's back, and drove him into the water. But DeGraff quickly used his dark magic to slip into the shadows, and Mr. Darby's hands struck the floor of the fountain.

When Mr. Darby stood back up, DeGraff was on the

street, water dripping from his trench coat and his hat missing. Traces of moonlight revealed his face like a hideous secret. His eyes and nose were empty sockets, and the flesh around his mouth looked like it had been torn away. He looked nothing like the man who had stood on Mr. Jackson's porch a hundred years ago. The magic in Mr. Darby's jacket had done much more to preserve his body.

"Come and get me, Mr. Jackson," said the creature standing in the street. He glanced around and saw what Mr. Darby did—the city was practically deserted, which meant DeGraff's army was almost finished being staged in the sectors. "Looks like it's almost time," DeGraff added as he smiled a heinous smile, the open wounds around his mouth spreading and exposing his black gum line.

"You're right," Mr. Darby said as he walked to the edge of the fountain and climbed out into the street. He needed to hold DeGraff off for a few more minutes to allow Noah and the others to complete their tasks. "It's almost time for you to die—something you and I should have done years ago."

CHAPTER 24

11:48

Noah continued to freefall, his arms and legs flailing. The two steep mountains were blurs at his sides, and the enormous drawbridge now seemed a sliver etched across the cloudy sky. Podgy was diving toward Noah, but he'd never be able to reach him in time.

Noah turned in the air and saw that the river was less than a hundred yards away. Landing in water wouldn't help from this height; he'd still be crushed by the impact. He closed his eyes and tried to accept what was about to happen. He was going to die, and the Primary Portal would never be activated. He wouldn't—

The curtain. He heard it fluttering and realized it was wrapped around his leg. An idea struck him. The curtain to Gator Falls had protected him from the jaws of an alligator. Could another curtain protect him now?

He spread the Primary Portal along his body. The velvet pressed against his front side—his stomach, his thighs, his face—and flapped in the air above him. Seconds later, the world suddenly went silent, and Noah felt water all around him. But he felt no pain. As the churning rapids pushed him through the surface of the river, he realized his idea had worked!

A wave struck his face, and the currents pulled him under. He stroked his arms and legs and surfaced again, drawing a deep breath. He glanced around at the raging river, the steep mountainsides, the distant drawbridge. He noticed something floating just off to his side: the curtain. He swam toward it with all his might, the rapids tossing his body about. He threw his arms over the curtain to keep it from getting away and was shocked when the next strong current didn't draw him under—the strange magic at work again.

Something appeared in front of him: a fallen tree that was partially rooted in the riverbed. As he was dragged beneath the trunk, he wrapped his arms around it. Then he hauled himself to land and crawled onto a muddy shore.

He barely caught his breath before realizing he didn't have the curtain. He looked out and saw it tangled in the branches of the tree. Time was running out, but if he hurried, he might still be able to set up the portal. He got to his feet, pushing through his fatigue and pain, and began to head for the river. A voice rose up behind him.

"Where you going, kid?"

Noah turned. Standing twenty feet away were Charlie Red and three sasquatches. Charlie's arms were freakishly long again. He had his baton, and he was swatting the fat end of it against his open palm. His eyes were now entirely red, even the parts that had once been white. Noah didn't know how he'd gotten down here so fast. A portal, perhaps.

"We've got some unfinished business," Charlie said.

Noah swept mud off his forehead. Then he pulled the cords on the straps of his backpack and prepared to fight.

CHAPTER 25

11:50

Mr. Darby looked around, his wet ponytail slipping across his shoulders. DeGraff had disappeared into the shadows again. Mr. Darby heard something rare in the City of Species: silence. No animals, no people. No rustle of windblown leaves, and no splash of water in the streams. The animals were in the sectors, ready for midnight.

Mr. Darby pulled out his gold pocket watch and opened the cover just as the second hand swept past the sixty-second mark and started a new minute: 11:50. The Secret Society had ten minutes to make Noah's plan work.

He returned his watch and moved in a slow circle. He saw fountains, trees, statues, but not the Shadowist.

"DeGraff!" he called out. "I'm here, old fool! Come and fight!"

He listened to his voice echo in the empty spaces between the buildings.

"He's gone," Mr. Darby softly spoke into his headset.

Jordynn said, "We don't see him, either."

Mr. Darby glanced in the general direction of the Crossers, but he couldn't make them out because of the mirage Jordynn had created.

"What do we do?" Ella asked.

Silence on the airwaves. Then Tank's voice: "We wait. We stick to the plan and hope DeGraff doesn't alter it."

More silence. Mr. Darby swept his gaze over the streets, hating what had become of his beloved city, and fearing what was about to become of Noah's world.

CHAPTER 26

11:51

Noah took a step toward Charlie, his tail dragging behind him. The sounds of the raging river echoed in the confined space of the ravine, drowning out the other background noise. The sasquatches began to spread out, grunting and growling and reaching their powerful arms out to their sides. Noah tried to think of everything he had learned from Sam. Now was the test, and the fate of two worlds was on the line. He tried to ignore his fears and concentrated on his hate for Charlie Red, knowing this was what a Descender would do.

"Get him!" Charlie commanded.

The sasquatches charged.

Noah spun, his thoughts and attention on the base of his spine, the place where Tameron's tail—*his* tail—magically connected. The fifteen-foot tail slid along the ground, slinging mud everywhere, and took out the legs of the sasquatches. The beasts fell over, sending tremors through the earth.

Noah's normal instincts kicked in, and he said, "Leave! Get out of here and I won't hurt you!"

But the sasquatches showed no signs of retreat. They stood and slowly advanced on Noah, their deadly claws ready to strike.

Noah thought of what Sam and Tameron and Hannah would do. They would attack. Descenders showed no mercy.

He swung his tail high over his head and brought it down on a sasquatch. The beast roared in pain and began to roll fitfully around in the mud, clutching its shoulder.

Don't hesitate, a voice spoke in Noah's head—a voice that was part Noah and part Sam, part scout and part Descender. *Finish it.*

He raised his tail again and brought it down with as much force as possible, just missing the sasquatch and splashing mud everywhere.

Something struck Noah's side, and stars flashed across his vision as he fell onto the ground. Charlie Red hovered over him. When Noah tried to get up, Charlie swung his baton and hit him again.

"Get him!" Charlie called out to the sasquatches. "Crush him!"

Noah rolled onto his back and saw that the two uninjured sasquatches were now standing by Charlie. He caught a glimpse of something on the river. Podgy. The penguin was floating by the fallen tree, stabbing at the Primary Portal with his bill, trying to free it from the branches. Noah also spotted Marlo darting back and forth

189

above the water.

Noah checked his watch: 11:51. Time was running out.

One of the sasquatches brought down its foot directly at Noah's head. Noah glimpsed the beast's plum-sized toes and then threw himself to one side, barely missing the blow. As Noah got to his feet, his tail dragged into place behind him. He pushed through the fog in his head and braced himself to fight. Two worlds needed him not to give up.

Charlie and the two sasquatches slowly spread out, forming a half circle around Noah. Charlie's oversized freckles looked like a terrible skin rash, and his red hair stood out in all directions, a messy mop with matted clumps. His hands dangled by his knees.

Noah glanced at Podgy. The penguin was still desperately tugging on the curtain, unable to free it. Charlie's gaze followed Noah's and he said, "Why is your fat friend so interested in that downed portal?"

Noah tensed up. He couldn't let Charlie know how important the portal was. He started to say something but stopped, fearing the wrong words might come out.

Charlie raised a bushy red eyebrow and studied Noah for a few seconds. Then, to one of the sasquatches, he said, "Get the curtain."

A sasquatch turned and ran for the river, its arms swinging at its sides.

"No!" Noah said, a bit surprised by his own voice. He

swung his tail parallel to the ground, four or five feet up. His tail hit the back of the sasquatch and launched it into the air. The beast splashed down in the river on the downstream side of the fallen tree, and the current dragged it off.

Podgy, looking frustrated, dove into the water and then surfaced a few feet away, his flippers fanning the air. He soared into the heights of the ravine—up and up toward the drawbridge, a shrinking black dot that soon blinked out.

Noah stood there, baffled. Under his breath, he said, "Podge, what are you doing?"

"Looks like your friend has better things to do," Charlie said with a crooked smile. "And now you're here all alone."

Noah stared at Charlie—his red eyes and the ugly splotches on his face. Then he checked his watch: 11:52.

"Kill him," Charlie said to the remaining sasquatch.

As the sasquatch charged, Charlie moved in simultaneously to attack. Noah readied himself again. He had just minutes to raise the portal, and Podgy, his only help, had deserted him.

CHAPTER 27

11:52

Mr. Darby fell forward so unexpectedly that he barely caught himself before he struck the cobblestone street. DeGraff had come out of nowhere—come out of the shadows, in fact. A boot pressed against the back of Mr. Darby's head, and his arms began to whip around. Just as he attempted to use one of his animal powers, his arms slipped out of his sleeves and he felt most of the magic purge from his body. DeGraff had taken his jacket.

He rolled over and saw DeGraff looming against the backdrop of the shadowy sky. A centipede crawled out of his empty eye socket, squirmed down his neck, and disappeared beneath the collar of his trench coat. As Mr. Darby stood, the Shadowist took a few steps and hurled the velvet jacket into a tree. Mr. Darby, knowing he'd never be able to quickly get to his jacket, took off running in the direction he thought Tank and the scouts were in. But before he could get far, DeGraff slipped into the shadows, appeared beside him, and knocked him to the street. Mr. Darby paused to catch his breath. After a few seconds, he tried to get up, but DeGraff shoved him down again.

A voice rose in his ear—the radio waves that he shared with the Crossers. Jordynn. "You're right by us. Thirty feet, and just to your left. Crawl if you have to."

Mr. Darby lifted himself to his hands and knees and began to move in the direction Jordynn had mentioned. He couldn't see her or any sign of what she'd done with her Specter powers.

"Mr. Jackson," DeGraff said, "I have something I want to share with you."

Mr. Darby didn't need to see DeGraff to know that he was referring to his knife.

"Crawl," Jordynn repeated over the airwaves. "You're almost here."

Mr. Darby did. As fast as he could.

CHAPTER 28

11:53

Ella could barely stand the pain in her hand. It felt like she had the hot tip of a match pressed to her palm. When she saw light seeping out between her fingers, she pressed them together.

"I can't hold on," Richie groaned, and Ella knew he was experiencing the same pain. Megan, too.

"You have to," Tank said, his voice just above a whisper, but loud and clear through the radio waves.

"Meg?" Ella said.

"I'm okay."

Ella turned back to the scene on the street. Mr. Darby was still crawling in their direction, and DeGraff was a few steps behind him, his knife held high.

"Tank?" Ella said into her headset. "Where are you?"

"About twenty feet behind DeGraff," Tank responded softly.

"Are you in position?"

"Yeah."

Ella looked at Mr. Darby again. "C'mon," she breathed. "Get closer."

CHAPTER 29

11:55

Noah quickly got to his feet, slipping in the mud. Then he faced Charlie and the sasquatch again. The three had been fighting for a minute, maybe more—time Noah didn't have. Movement at the top of the ravine caught his attention. He looked up and saw a strange cloud of dots above the drawbridge. As the cloud began to drift down between the mountainsides, Noah realized that the dots were hundreds of hummingbirds. Leading them was a much larger bird—a penguin.

"Podgy..." Noah breathed.

As the hummingbirds reached the base of the ravine, they began to hover directly above the Primary Portal, grabbing it with their tiny talons. Once hundreds of the birds had a hold, they started to fly upward, slowly lifting the curtain.

Noah checked his watch: 11:55. Five minutes for all the pieces of his plan to come together. It wasn't enough time.

Charlie seemed to realize what was happening, and as he ran for the river, Noah knocked him and the sasquatch over with his tail. Charlie snarled. Then he jumped to his feet, favoring his right leg, and said to the sasquatch, "Get the curtain. I'll take care of the Descender."

Descender. Noah wasn't a Descender—he was a boy from a group of childhood friends. But as Noah moved and felt the weight of the massive tail behind him, he wondered what was true.

The sasquatch knuckle-walked to the edge of the river, out of reach of Noah's tail.

"C'mon, *Descender*," Charlie said, and this time he used the term in a mocking way. "In a couple minutes, this will all be over. Your world is about to become ours."

Charlie sidestepped to his left, his grotesque arms out to his sides. Behind him, the hummingbirds continued to work on freeing the curtain.

Use your pain to focus, a voice inside Noah said. And though it was Sam's voice, it was sounding more and more like his own.

Noah thought of everything he'd endured in the past year. He thought of when his sister was missing, the battles he'd lost in the Secret Zoo, and being forced to lie to his parents, who might now be gone forever. He allowed his pain to become anger, and then he lashed out with his tail.

Charlie easily avoided the blow this time. Then he charged Noah and swung his baton, connecting with Noah's head. Noah fell, his ear ringing and pain shooting from his temple. As he struck the ground, his view of the world turned sideways, and he happened to see the commotion in the river. The hummingbirds almost had the Primary Portal off the tree, but the sasquatch was knee-deep in the water, quickly closing in.

CHAPTER 30

11:56

Crawl, Mr. Darby, crawl.

Ella wasn't sure if she'd spoken the words or only thought them.

DeGraff was now standing above Mr. Darby, one leg on each side of his torso, the end of his trench coat draped across the old man's legs. His steel knife was raised high, ready to strike.

The burn in Ella's palm was stronger than ever, but she barely cared. Mr. Darby was the only thing that mattered.

"Roll!" someone commanded across the airwaves. Jordynn.

Mr. Darby did as instructed, and as he rolled against the inside of DeGraff's leg, the Shadowist came down with the knife, which barely missed its target and got wedged between two blocks in the cobblestone street. It took a few seconds for DeGraff to free it, and by that time, Mr. Darby had been able to crawl out from under him, get up, and take off running.

"Veer left!" Jordynn said, and Mr. Darby did. The old man staggered as he ran. Without his jacket, he was getting slower and weaker.

"I can't hold this thing!" Richie said over the airwaves.

Ella looked around the room. Richie and Megan were standing just a few feet away, each with a fist held out. Jordynn had her arms out to her sides and all her attention on controlling the mirage she'd created.

The mirage. The idea for it had come to Noah when he'd been staring into the City of Species from his kitchen and noticed Lots of Latte, the quaint coffee shop standing by itself on one end of a street.

"Can you hide it?" Noah had asked Jordynn, and then pointed to what the chameleons had done to the wall between his kitchen and living room. "Like that?"

Jordynn had looked at the coffee shop. "The entire building?"

Noah had nodded, looking more serious and hopeful than Ella had ever seen him look.

Jordynn had continued to stare at Lots of Latte, considering it. "It's big," she'd said at last. "A mirage would work best. Mask the outside walls instead of ghosting everything inside."

"So you can do it?"

"I can try."

The mirage had worked perfectly. Hundreds of chameleons had crawled onto the roof and along the outside walls of the coffee shop, using their magic to conceal the small building and everything inside it, while allowing the people indoors to see things like normal.

Now Ella looked around at the fireflies in Lots of Latte. There were hundreds, maybe thousands. The scouts had used their Specter pants to draw them out of the Institute of Light once Lee-Lee had positioned the flour sacks from the old bakery on the Streets of Transparency in the museum. Now the Specter pants transferred fireflies instead of chameleons. Lee-Lee had moved the magical flour sacks after the scouts had drawn out enough chameleons to hide the coffee shop.

"Ella...I can't..."

"A few more seconds!" Megan chimed in. She was by the door, one hand on the knob.

Richie screamed, and it was a horrifying, primal sound: *"Rrraahhgghh!"* His fingers opened and light burst from his hand. The firefly nearest to him exploded with light, and then so did the second closest, the third, the fourth—on and on, a chain reaction like the one Noah had talked about seeing in the Institute of Light.

Ella closed her eyes against the blinding light and did the only thing she could. She rolled open her fingers and released her attack.

CHAPTER 31

11:57

Mr. Darby heard the scream and knew at once that it had been Richie. He glanced over his shoulder and saw that DeGraff was no longer chasing him—he was standing still in the street, staring toward the hidden coffee shop just beyond Mr. Darby.

"DeGraff!" Mr. Darby shouted, knowing he had to draw his nemesis closer.

The Shadowist looked at him, and then returned his gaze to the empty place where the scream had originated.

No! Mr. Darby thought. *I'm here! Come after me!*

The grotesque features of DeGraff's face suddenly became fully visible—his empty eye sockets, his missing flesh—and Mr. Darby realized light was coming from somewhere. He turned and saw what DeGraff did. Light seemed to be coming out of the nothingness in the street, thin beams giving off a dim glow. Mr. Darby knew what he hoped DeGraff didn't—that the light was coming from inside Lots of Latte, bursting through gaps between the boards in the walls.

"DeGraff!" Mr. Darby yelled in panic. "Fight me while

I'm standing!"

But Mr. Darby could tell by the new focus of DeGraff's gaze—his sudden lack of interest in Mr. Darby—that he'd realized he was being led into a trap.

CHAPTER 32

11:57

The sasquatch, still knee-deep in the water, reached out and grabbed the Primary Portal. He tried to pull it away from the hummingbirds, but the hundreds of tiny birds—their strength in their number—resisted.

"No!" Noah yelled, and he charged the river. But before he could get more than a few steps, Charlie knocked him down. Noah curled his tail around Charlie's ankles and pulled him to the ground. Then he jumped back up. The sasquatch suddenly buckled over as something struck its stomach: a large black bird with thin wings—wings, Noah knew, that were actually flippers. Podgy. The sasquatch lost its hold on the Primary Portal and splashed down in the shallow edge of the river. Podgy skipped across the water and then slid along the muddy shore.

Noah, realizing Charlie was trying to get up, lifted his tail high and said, "Don't!"

Charlie didn't.

The sasquatch that Podgy had plowed into was writhing in the water, its long hair swaying in the current. The hummingbirds, looking like hundreds of colorful tassels, lifted the curtain up and off the fallen tree.

Noah checked his watch: 11:57. There was no way the hummingbirds could make it to the courtyard in time. He glanced around for a safe place to hang the curtain and didn't see one—only the two ravines, the one above the river and the one he and Charlie were standing in.

CHAPTER 33

11:58

Tank stared at the thin beams of light shooting across the street. They appeared to be coming from nowhere, but he knew the truth. The light was emitting from Lots of Latte—from the fireflies the scouts had released from the portals in their Specter pants. It was part of Noah's plan—it just wasn't supposed to happen quite yet.

Tank had been secretly following Mr. Darby and DeGraff on the street, waiting for the right moment to act. Chameleons were still clinging to his body, providing him with perfect camouflage. Now he was less than twenty feet behind DeGraff, who was standing still, all his attention on the light instead of Mr. Darby.

DeGraff was about to escape into the shadows again—Tank was sure of it. Needing to improvise, Tank touched the transmit button on his headset and softly said, "Open the door. Now."

A pause, and then Megan said, "But Mr. Darby's not—"

"*Now*," Tank said, his voice firm but quiet so DeGraff wouldn't hear.

The front door of the coffee shop suddenly flew open, and a rectangle of blinding light appeared on the shadowy street. As the world turned bright white, Tank charged, his arms out to his sides. He headed for the place he hoped DeGraff was still standing, and a second later, his chest struck the small of DeGraff's back. He wrapped his arms around DeGraff's torso and hoisted him onto his shoulder. Then he closed his eyes and ran—he ran like he never had in his life, trusting that the position of the coffee shop entrance was still straight ahead.

"*Arrhhh!*" he screamed, all his emotion bleeding out in a single, meaningless sound. He had captured DeGraff, at least for the moment.

His free shoulder struck something solid—the frame of the doorway. He felt a board break away, and then he spun and tumbled across the threshold of the coffee shop. DeGraff slipped off his shoulder and cried out in pain—not because of his impact with the floor, Tank knew, but because of the bright, continuous light.

Tank tried to open his eyes, but the room was too blinding. He felt his body being peppered by small objects— fireflies, he realized, a countless number. He felt around the floor with one foot, located DeGraff, and dropped down onto him, driving his knees into his back.

"I'm releasing the mirage!" Jordynn said.

"Please do," a voice said. Mr. Darby. Though Tank

couldn't see him, he knew the old man was now standing at the front entrance.

Tank heard footsteps, slow and deliberate. Then he sensed Mr. Darby standing beside him.

"DeGraff, old friend," Mr. Darby said. "Can you hear me?"

DeGraff continued to cry out in pain.

Mr. Darby said, "Tank, can you please repeat the question?"

Tank, knowing what this meant, drove his knees down harder on DeGraff's back.

"*ARRGGHH!*" DeGraff howled. "Yes, yes, I can hear you!" His voice was barely more than a gurgle in his throat.

"I want you to call off the attack," Mr. Darby said.

DeGraff managed to laugh. "I don't think so."

"Once you're gone, your spell on the animals will end."

"How can you know?"

"Because Noah has been paying attention."

DeGraff tried to break free. Tank could feel DeGraff's strength weakening as the light continued to draw the life from his body.

After a few seconds, Mr. Darby said, "This is for Marlo, Blizzard, Sam—each and every Secret Cityzen."

"I created the Secret Zoo," DeGraff uttered. "It's mine."

"You're wrong," Mr. Darby said. "It's Frederick's. It

207

always has been."

DeGraff howled in pain and squirmed beneath Tank, more feeble than ever.

"And I won't let you have it," Mr. Darby added.

The fireflies continued to explode with light. Seconds passed. And then a minute. DeGraff became silent. And then he became more and more still.

CHAPTER 34

11:59

Noah noticed that the ravine was getter brighter and brighter. He looked toward the top of the mountainside and saw light filtering through the curtain to the City of Species. On the drawbridge, the small group of sasquatches was scattering, and even with the distance and the noisy river, Noah could hear their howls. He had no doubt that the light was coming from the fireflies at Lots of Latte.

"What's…what's going on?" Charlie nervously asked as he, too, saw the light. He was still lying on the ground, Noah's tail hovering above him. "What are you up to?"

Noah turned to Charlie and saw that his arms were almost back to their natural length, and his eyes weren't as red. DeGraff, Noah realized, was being doused in the firefly light.

He filled with hope and glanced at his watch just as 11:58 became 11:59. One minute was all he had. He looked out at the river. The hummingbirds were still holding the Primary Portal just above the water. Combined, they were stronger than Noah could have imagined. And with that realization came an idea.

Noah turned to Marlo, who was perched on his shoulder again, and said, "The hummingbirds—tell them to turn the curtain toward me, away from the river."

Marlo sprang from Noah's shoulder and flew to the hummingbirds. He darted back and forth along the top edge of the curtain, chirping wildly. After a few seconds, the hummingbirds slowly swung the Primary Portal around like a door to face Noah and Charlie. The curtain, perhaps thirty feet away, stopped short of the sides of the ravine, allowing space for an escape.

"Kid—what are you *doing*?" Charlie asked, a quiver in his voice.

Noah reached into his jacket pocket and pulled out the mod. Then he held it in one hand so that Charlie could see. "This," he said, and he pressed the button.

For a moment, Noah worried that the Multipoint wouldn't work. But then the Primary Portal began to ripple and sway as the wind from all the Secret Zoo sectors pushed against it. And then Noah heard something. A rumble—the sound of a stampede.

Charlie, his eyes still faintly glowing red, jumped to his feet and fixed his gaze on the Primary Portal. He took a step back. Then another, and another.

"All the gateways in the Clarksville Zoo have been recalibrated," Noah said. Then he nodded to the Primary Portal, adding, "They're all joined here."

"No," Charlie said, shaking his head. "That's impossible!"

"Then what's that sound?"

Charlie listened. The rumble of the stampede grew louder and louder.

Noah took off running for the other side of the portal, wondering if he could make it in time and nervously watching for the first animal to break through.

CHAPTER 35

11:59

Ella opened one eye. The fireflies were dimming, and she could see things. A long countertop, tables and chairs, a row of large coffeemakers. Lots of Latte. People were standing around—her friends, Jordynn, and Mr. Darby. Hundreds of fireflies dotted the air, spots of softening light. Tank was kneeling, and Ella saw a scattering of things around and beneath him: a trench coat, a fedora hat, boots, gloves—and a stark white skeleton.

"Tank?" Ella said.

Colors began to bleed back into the world. Ella walked over to Tank and stood beside him to take a closer look at what remained of DeGraff, the man-creature who had haunted the Secret Zoo for nearly a hundred years.

As the dimming firefly light continued to shine, the skeleton beneath Tank began to crack and turn to dust—dust that flew out from openings in the coat and blew away in the breeze from the open door. Bone dust swirled into the air and shined like dust captured in a slant of morning sunlight. A thin, continuous layer blew off DeGraff's skull. The skull thinned and thinned, and then a cavity opened in the bone and began to elongate. The hole joined to the other sockets—the eyes and nose—and then the skull collapsed, yellow teeth clicking against the hard floor. All the elevated spots in DeGraff's clothes—the places where his bones were—flattened. In little more than a minute, DeGraff's entire skeleton was gone.

The floorboards creaked as Richie, Megan, and Jordynn walked up, leaving faint footprints in the bone dust. Mr. Darby, who was already standing next to Tank, stared down at the jacket, the hat, the gloves. Tank looked up at the old man, and Ella could hear the question in his gaze—it was the same question everyone in the room had.

Mr. Darby squatted and picked up the fedora. He turned it in his hand, studying its details. Then he let it fall from his grip. He glanced at everyone. Then he touched the transmit button on his headset.

"Anyone there?"

"I'm here," Sam answered, and Ella heard his voice in her ear. "I'm still outside Teknikal Tower. The storm…it's starting to clear!"

"Sam, I need you to do something."

"What is it?" Sam asked.

"I need you to gather our troops and let them know that DeGraff is dead."

The airwaves fell silent. Ella realized she was holding her breath.

"Are you…are you sure?" Sam asked.

Mr. Darby lifted the empty sleeve of DeGraff's trench coat, and more dust fell through the opening. "Quite certain," he said.

"Roger!" Sam shouted, his voice pulsing with energy.

Mr. Darby looked at Ella, Richie, Megan, Jordynn. Then he put his hand on Tank's shoulder, and one side of his mouth curled up in a smile. "He's gone," he said. "The Shadowist is no more."

Ella traded glances with Richie and Megan. Then the three friends ran into one another's arms. Ella felt her chest shudder, and tears blurred her sight. She began to cry, and she didn't care that everyone could see her.

It was over. Almost.

CHAPTER 36

THE STRIKE OF TWELVE

The rumble of the stampede continued to grow louder and louder. The animals would soon push through the curtain and charge across the ravine, trampling everything in their path, including Noah and Charlie if they couldn't get around the portal.

Noah ran as fast as he could, his tail dragging behind him, mud splashing everywhere. The curtain came to within twenty feet, ten. The velvet continued to ripple and sway, and Noah heard the sounds of rhinos, lions, and elephants—all the animals from all the sectors of the Secret Zoo. He dodged the curtain and ran onto the small shore between the portal and the raging river.

He looked around for Charlie, prepared to defend himself. But when Charlie didn't appear, he glanced back and saw the former security guard from the Clarksville Zoo standing in the middle of the ravine.

"Charlie!" Noah called out.

Charlie looked up. His eyes were almost white, and his splotchy freckles were close to their normal size. Charlie was coming out from under DeGraff's spell—he was becoming human again.

"My foot!" Charlie said, and Noah could barely hear his voice because the sound of the stampede had grown so loud, amplifying and echoing in the narrow ravine. Charlie tried to pull his body in one direction. "It's…it's *stuck!*"

Noah instinctively took a step toward him, and then stopped.

Don't, a voice inside him said. *His life is not worth risking yours. Besides, he's the enemy.*

Charlie had been against the scouts since the beginning, even before he fell under DeGraff's dark magic. When Megan was missing, he'd helped keep her whereabouts a secret, and he'd tried everything to stop the scouts from discovering the Secret Zoo. He was definitely one of the bad guys, human or not.

"Noah!" Charlie called out. "C'mon, man—help!"

No, the voice inside Noah said. *Descenders show no mercy.*

But Noah's heart told him something different. Charlie was a person, and good or bad, he didn't deserve to die like this. To show mercy was to show strength.

Noah made up his mind. He dashed toward Charlie, skimming the curtain as he passed it. The sounds of the stampede seemed to echo in his head. He glanced back and saw the curtain swaying more than ever, revealing glimpses of an approaching animal herd. When he reached Charlie, he saw that his foot was wedged between several rocks that were partially buried in the mud.

"I can't get it out!" Charlie said, his voice slurring with panic.

Noah dropped to one knee, grabbed the bottom of Charlie's leg, and pulled. Nothing.

The sounds of the animals were now nearly deafening—their grunts, their growls, their footfalls.

Noah jumped up and moved a few steps away from Charlie, saying, "Can you swim?"

Charlie stared at Noah, confused. *"What?"*

"Can you swim?"

Charlie thought about it for a few seconds—not the question, but why Noah was asking it, Noah guessed. *"Yes!"*

Noah nodded. Then he raised his tail a few feet off the ground, saying, "I'm sorry if this hurts!" He turned and wrapped the last few feet of his tail around Charlie's waist like he'd learned to do in the Institute of Light. Then he took a step and pulled. Charlie's foot came free, and Charlie splashed down in the mud several feet away, Noah's tail still coiled around his midsection. Noah then turned and swung his tail high above his head, pitching Charlie into the air. Charlie, his arms and legs flailing, flew over the Primary Portal, startling the hummingbirds, and then splashed into the river.

Before Noah could run for safety again, the curtain flew

open and dozens of rhinos charged out, immediately spreading to the edges of the ravine. Noah froze. There was nowhere for him to go—no way to escape.

·

CHAPTER 37

LAST-DITCH EFFORT

As Noah stood and stared at the stampede, something drifted down just inches from his face and landed near his feet. A leaf. A second leaf touched down, and then a third and a fourth. Noah noticed a few twigs resting on top of the mud—they hadn't been there a moment ago. He glanced up and saw the limbs of a tree that was growing out sideways from the wall of the ravine. When Noah had thrown Charlie to safety, the end of his tail had brushed against the branches. The tree was within reach.

New hope swelled in Noah. With only seconds to act, he swung his tail over his head and was able to curl the last few feet of it around an overhead limb. The first rhino in the stampede fixed his eyes on Noah, and as he got close, Noah jumped and planted both feet on the animal's head. As the rhinoceros continued to plow forward, Noah pushed off with his legs and swung into the air, his tail still wrapped around the limb. Up and around he went, the growing herd of rhinos passing beneath him. He came level with the limb and then swung into the dense part of the tree, a mesh of limbs and leaves. He grabbed onto a thick branch, secured himself, and

219

allowed his tail to slip free. Then he closed his eyes and caught his breath, feeling a wave of relief wash over him.

After a few seconds, he looked down at the tops of the rhinos as dozens charged past. The thuds of their weighty hooves boomed in the hollow space of the ravine and shook the tree, making the leaves tremble. Noah studied their eyes and realized something: Their color was normal. And then he noticed something else: The rhinos' horns and bodies were back to their normal size. DeGraff's dark magic had left them.

"He's…he's dead," Noah said under his breath. "DeGraff—he's gone."

It took a few seconds for this to sink in. Then Noah felt like he would burst with joy and new relief. His plan, as outlandish as it had seemed, had worked. He thrust a fist into the air and screamed as loud as he could—a loud, primal sound that might have blended with the animal calls in the Secret Zoo. A tear trickled from the corner of his eye and streaked through the mud on his face. The Shadowist was dead, his dark hold on the animals was no more, and Noah's world had been saved along with the Secret Zoo.

Other animals began to charge across the Multipoint. Elephants, lions, bears—animals from all the sectors in the Secret Zoo. They all looked normal, just in a panic because of the stampede, which showed no signs of letting up.

He felt something on his shoulder and turned to see

Marlo perched in his normal spot. The bright blue kingfisher jumped into the air, circled a few branches, and then darted off. Noah watched as he landed on a nearby ledge of the mountainside, the place where the tree Noah was in was rooted, and the place where Podgy was standing. The emperor penguin met Noah's gaze and wagged his flippers once. His intentions were clear: He wanted to fly Noah out of the ravine.

Noah pulled the cords on his shoulder straps and retracted his tail. Then he carefully climbed along the limb he'd landed on. At the trunk of the tree, he stood and walked, holding the branches for support, mindful that his life depended on not slipping—the stampede below would crush him in an instant. At the mountainside, he stepped onto the rocky ledge, which was barely big enough for Podgy and Noah to stand, and took a deep, needed breath.

Podgy turned his back to Noah, inviting him to hang on. Noah looked over the ledge and saw the stampede about fifteen feet below. He put his arms around the penguin and said, "Let's go."

Podgy dropped from the mountainside like it was Noah's bedroom window, and leveled out just a few feet above the stampede. He swerved around the long necks of giraffes and skimmed the backs of lions. As he flew over the Primary Portal, Noah watched the hummingbirds hold up the curtain, something they would continue to do until the stampede ended.

With Marlo following, Podgy swept into the heights of the ravine, over the raging river, and up toward the drawbridge where the sasquatches were still standing, looking as ordinary as sasquatches could. They were free from DeGraff's wicked magic, just like everything else in the Secret Zoo.

CHAPTER 38

MOMENTS AFTER MIDNIGHT

Podgy took the shortcut through the Forest of Flight and then turned onto the same street where they'd started. Lots of Latte was in plain view, which meant the mirage was down. Thousands of fireflies speckled the air, and chameleons crawled all around. People were standing outside the coffee shop—Jordynn, Ella, Megan, Richie, Tank, and Mr. Darby, who was feeding his arms through the sleeves of his velvet jacket, looking sore and tired. Podgy touched down beside the group, and Noah stepped away from the perfect landing as Marlo landed on his shoulder.

Tank held up a trench coat and a fedora for Noah to see. "He's dead."

Noah scanned his friends' expressions. "Are you sure?"

Tank smiled and nodded. "We saw his bones turn to dust. And look…" Tank pointed to the sky. "The storm is clearing."

Noah looked up and saw clouds beginning to shine beneath new starlight.

"The Multipoint!" Ella said to Noah. "What happened?"

"It worked!" Noah said, and then he told them about his improvisation—how the hummingbirds were holding up the Primary Portal in the ravine. "The animals are coming through, and they all look normal."

"Noah!" Megan blurted as she pointed to a place behind him. "Mom and Dad!"

Noah spun around and saw his parents being led their way by two of the security guards from Noah's house. They'd come from a building down the street—a makeshift prison, it seemed. The guards, like Charlie Red and the animals, were out from under DeGraff's spell. When Mr. and Mrs. Nowicki spotted their children, they ran over and wrapped Noah and Megan in their arms.

"Are you okay?" Mrs. Nowicki asked as she held Megan's shoulders and looked her over. "Your hands!" she said, noticing the firefly wounds on both Megan and Noah's palms.

"It's nothing," Megan said. "Are you hurt?"

Mrs. Nowicki shook her head. "Those men…" she said, pointing to the guards. "They took us. They…" She suddenly glanced around, as if she'd just noticed the city. "Where…where are we?"

Mr. Darby answered. "The Secret Zoo."

"The secret *what*?"

"The City of Species," Mr. Darby said. "A place just beyond your world."

Mrs. Nowicki looked around at the group and seemed to consider this. "I don't…I don't understand."

"Magic," Megan said. "Magic created this place."

"But magic isn't real."

"Tell that to this one," Mr. Darby said, and he gestured to Blizzard, who had charged across the street to join the group. Noah's parents jumped back as Blizzard strolled up to Noah.

"It's okay," Noah said as he put his hand on Blizzard's back. "He's our friend."

Mrs. Nowicki stared at Blizzard, wide-eyed, and gently shook her head. "He's…he's a *bear*."

"And this guy's a penguin," Ella said, gesturing to Podgy. "A big one. He flies, too, which is pretty cool."

Mrs. Nowicki shook her head again. A thought seemed to strike her, and she lowered her gaze at Megan. "Is this where you disappeared to? Those three weeks—were you here?"

Megan nodded. "I'm sorry we lied. We had to. And then we had to keep so many secrets from you and Dad. It never felt right, but we didn't have a choice."

Her mother looked around and seemed to consider all this. After a few seconds, she said, "Volunteering at the zoo?"

Megan shook her head. "We made it up." She told her mother about joining the Secret Society as Crossers, and then she explained what Crossers did.

Mrs. Nowicki stared at the sights again. She started to say something more, and then stopped.

Noah looked past his parents, saw the security guards again, and thought of Charlie Red. He told the group what had happened to Charlie—how Noah had saved his life by throwing him into the river.

"We'll deal with him," Mr. Darby said. "Justly." Then he touched the transmit button on his headset and ordered a group of Descenders to search for Charlie.

A coterie of prairie dogs scurried up and started sniffing the ground, a few paying particular attention to Richie's flashy running shoes, the way they often did. When P-Dog stood up on his haunches by Ella, she leaned over and patted his head.

"It's over, P!" Ella said. "We did it!"

P-Dog sniffed the air, and Noah wondered if a world without DeGraff had a different smell.

Sam joined the group, along with Tameron, who was leaning on his friend for support. Hannah ran up, too. They were smiling and looking relieved, and Noah realized they'd already gotten the news.

Secret Cityzens were reentering the city from various places in the Secret Zoo—buildings, sectors, and houses just beyond the outskirts of the city. Parents and children were hugging one another and staring into the sky, which continued to clear. Some started to dance, and small fireworks began to go off, streaking color across the night and startling birds out of the trees.

Zak appeared, along with a few other Teknikals, young adults with wild haircuts and electrical gadgets clipped to their hips. They looked like geeks from another world, which, Noah realized, they pretty much were.

"Awesome work," Zak said to Noah, and he held out his hand toward him, not for a handshake or a high five, but something in between.

Noah half clapped and half shook Zak's hand. "It worked. The Multipoint—it worked just like you said it would."

Zak winked. "That's what the Teks do, bro. We make things work."

"Hannah," Mr. Darby said, "please gather a crew of Crossers who live on the Outside and have them make sure no animals are loose in Clarksville. Now that DeGraff's magic is gone, they should be able to take down the portals to Earth. Have them decommission all the portals but the one in Noah's kitchen. Commence with Operation Division and quickly come back."

Hannah nodded. Then she looked at the scouts, a hint of sadness in her eyes, and ran off.

Noah turned to Mr. Darby, who must have seen his concern, because he said, "The portals are essentially broken now, Noah—remember what we talked about." As he watched Hannah leave, he added, "Besides, this is the best way, the safest way."

Noah wondered if the safest way was always the best, but he kept quiet.

Mrs. Nowicki said, "I don't...I don't understand. All the *portals*? What are you talking about?"

As Mr. Darby started to explain, Richie pointed off into the distance, shouting, "Look! The animals!"

Different animals were coming through the gateway to Koala Kastle, an internal portal that hadn't been affected by the Multipoint. They'd found a way to get up the mountainside. Various species quickly crowded the street, and as the night sky continued to brighten, the City of Species began to look the way it once had, like an enchanting place from a child's daydream.

More fireworks boomed. Music had started playing, and more people were dancing. Children began to ride the animals.

Little Bighorn appeared, gently nudging Ella with his enormous snout. Ella laughed and hugged the better part of his massive neck.

"Ella," Mrs. Nowicki said, "your mother...does she know about this place?"

Ella shook her head. "We're the only ones. And you—you and Mr. Nowicki."

228

"I'll have to tell her. Richie's parents, too."

"That won't be necessary," Mr. Darby said. "Our adventure together has come to a close."

Noah stared at Mr. Darby, feeling pride because they'd won, but sadness, too.

"It doesn't have to be," Megan suddenly said. "DeGraff is gone, but there are more ways we can help."

Mr. Darby smiled and shook his head. "You have already given us more than we could have asked for."

"Yeah, but we—"

"The Secret Society would have to build a new portal to your world, one for only you and your friends. I don't think that's wise now, Megan. We can operate as we once did to conserve animals—in individual groups. I think the time has come for you to return to your lives. Fully. Your world needs you. I know your parents would agree."

Mrs. Nowicki nodded. "Megan…we need you home." She gazed at the city again. "I don't know what this place is…but you can't stay here."

"I don't want to *stay*, Mom. I just wish I could come back. Once in a while." Her voice wavered with emotion. "We have friends here. Family."

Mr. Darby smiled. "Dear Megan, I know how you feel. Good-bye is never easy, not for anyone."

Blizzard strolled over to Megan and forced his snout under her hand so that she would pet him. Noah's mom, seeing this, took a step toward Blizzard and then stopped, and Noah could tell she was trying to convince herself that her daughter was safe.

Podgy walked over to Noah and stood close. He seemed to understand that the scouts were preparing for their final good-byes.

"Megan," Mr. Nowicki said, "I'm your father." He put his hand on his wife's shoulder and added, "We're your parents. Whatever this place is—no matter how... *incredible* it is—we have to keep you safe. We have to do that because it's our responsibility. And because we love you."

Noah glanced at Podgy, P-Dog, Blizzard. He could see sadness in the eyes of his animal companions.

Richie kneeled and more than a dozen prairie dogs tried to climb up his legs. Richie started petting them, doing his best to give them equal time. Then he picked up P-Dog and held him tight.

"Maybe you could put our animal friends in the Clarksville Zoo!" Richie said, his voice filled with hope. "You know—Blizzard, Little Bighorn, Podgy. Maybe they could come home with us!"

Mr. Darby smiled a sad smile. "They're Gifteds, Richie. They belong here, with the magic."

Noah sensed a larger crowd gathering. He looked over his shoulder and saw more people and animals all around. They'd come to see the scouts leave their world for the final

230

time.

"It's okay, dear," Mr. Darby said to Ella, who was crying and hugging Little Bighorn. Noah felt a swirl of emotions as memories of adventures with their rhino friend flashed in his head. Storming into the Dark Lands, the police standoff in Clarksville Elementary, the rescue from the zoo that he and Blizzard had been transferred to. Little Bighorn had been with the scouts since the day they discovered the Secret Zoo.

"Hey!" Ella said, and she chuckled as tears continued to stream down her cheeks. Ko, the koala she'd befriended in Koala Kastle, had climbed onto her back.

Tank started to laugh—a deep, booming sound that reminded Noah of the fireworks being set off.

"I can't take you with me, Ko," Ella said as she gently pried the koala off her back and then set her on the ground. "Not this time."

There won't be another time, Noah thought. He felt an animal climbing up his leg, and he looked down to see Louie, the otter that had clung to him when Noah had ridden the glass slide from the Wotter Park. Noah laughed and stroked Louie's long back. The otter, apparently satisfied, returned to the noisy crowd, moonlight gleaming on his sleek fur.

Mr. and Mrs. Nowicki stood by, pulling away from animals that were too close.

"It's a dream," Noah's father said to his mother.

Noah smiled. "We all thought that, Dad."

His father cupped his hand behind his ear to show he hadn't heard.

Noah continued to smile. "Never mind."

A firefly touched down on Noah's sleeve. It blinked once, twice—quick spots of yellow light. Noah wondered if the insect had any idea of what it and the other fireflies had just accomplished. He softly closed his uninjured hand around the firefly, watched it blink once, and then gently tossed it into the air just as another burst of fireworks went off in the distance.

Sam turned to Noah. He adjusted his leather jacket and said, "This is it, huh? This is good-bye?"

"Yeah," Noah said. "I guess so."

The silence that followed was weighty and awkward. Noah tried to hold Sam's gaze, but couldn't. When he reached out his hand for the Descender to shake, Sam grabbed it and pulled Noah in for a hug. Then he backed away, saying, "Thanks for all your help."

Noah thought of something. "The patrols. Of the Clarksville Zoo. Do you think—"

Sam shook his head. "Not after Operation Division. We'll stay on the Inside." He half frowned and half smiled. Then he stepped back to give someone else a turn with Noah.

All the Specters except Evie pushed through the crowd

and walked up to say their good-byes. Ella hugged each of them and then said something that made the five girls laugh.

Richie, noticing this, stepped forward. "I don't get it—why does she make you laugh so much?"

Elakshi said, "Ah...because she's funny."

"Funny? *She's* funny?" He turned directly to the Specters and said, "All right, see if you get this one." He cleared his throat and added, "What's white...and furry...and shaped like a tooth?"

The Specters traded empty glances. Elakshi shrugged.

Richie waited a few seconds and then trumpeted, "A *molar* bear!"

No one laughed. The only sounds were the noisy crowd and the booming fireworks. Richie looked at the Descenders, and then at his friends. "So it's really not funny?" he asked, sounding surprised.

Elakshi smiled. "It's cute." Then she leaned forward and planted a quick kiss on Richie's cheek. "Like you."

Richie's face turned as red as his hat. He took a quick step back as everyone laughed.

The scouts spent the next fifteen minutes or so saying good-bye to the Specters, the Descenders, and the animals they'd shared adventures with. When they were approached by Daisy, the ape who'd helped them get into the Secret Zoo, Noah remembered how he and his friends had crossed Metr-APE-olis by swinging from the hands of apes in the tall trees. When a swarm of chickadees flew around them, Noah thought of when the small birds had welcomed the scouts to the Secret Society by carrying them above the streets. When a goliath frog hopped up, Noah recalled the time the enormous frogs had saved them from the sasquatches in Pollywog Bog.

"I don't want to go," Richie said, and Noah realized his best friend was talking to him. "I mean...I *do* want to go...just not forever."

"I know," Noah said. He thought of all their animal friends and added, "I don't want to, either." He had to raise his voice to be heard over the celebration going on in the city.

"It's like coming to the end of a fairy tale," Megan said, and Noah realized she and Ella were listening. "Who wants that?"

"You can't leave this fairy tale behind," Mr. Darby spoke up. Noah felt a surge of hope, and then realized Mr. Darby probably wasn't being literal. Sure enough, he added, "This fairy tale is a part of you now—it helped shape who you are." The old man looked at each of them and then settled his gaze on Richie. "This one especially, I think."

Mr. Darby was right. In the beginning, Richie had hated almost everything about the Secret Zoo. He'd been afraid of heights, of water, and of almost all the animals. But just minutes ago, he'd helped defeat DeGraff.

Mr. Darby stepped up to Richie and gripped his shoulder. "Don't forget how brave you can be, young man."

Noah expected Richie to respond with a witty remark. Instead, Richie nodded and said, "I won't."

Mr. Darby turned to Ella. "And you…" he said as he set his open hand over her heart. "Don't be afraid to let your kindness show. It's the finest part of who you are."

Ella smiled, nodded, and wiped back a fresh tear.

Mr. Darby moved his attention to Megan. "Your adventurous spirit helped right the Secret Zoo, young lady. I don't doubt that it can do the same for your world."

Megan smiled and briefly touched Mr. Darby's hand.

Just then, Hannah walked up. "It's done," she said. "There aren't any animals loose in Clarksville. And the Outside Crossers already rounded up the ones in Noah's school and sent them back. Every exhibit at the Clarksville Zoo has the normal number of animals."

"Excellent!" Mr. Darby said. "And the portals?"

"The Crossers have started taking them down. They found the one in Noah's school and took care of it."

Noah traded an uneasy look with his friends. A part of him wanted to stop what was happening, but he knew he couldn't.

Mr. Darby stood tall and said, "Scouts—it sounds like it's time for the four of you to return home."

Noah looked at his friends again and saw something he

235

hadn't noticed before now: fatigue. Their eyes were dark and glassy, and their shoulders were slumped. He thought of his bed and a good night's rest without the worry of DeGraff prowling his neighborhood. Then he thought of home, and of how long he'd had a foot in two worlds, never being fully present in either. It would be good to feel whole again.

Ella nodded. And then so did Megan and Richie. It was clear that it was time to leave the Secret Zoo, once more and forever. Noah turned to Mr. Darby and softly said, "We're ready."

Mr. Darby's forced smile revealed that he had mixed feelings, too. He lightly poked Noah's chest and said, "What do you plan to do with that?"

Noah was confused until he looked down and saw the straps of his backpack. "Oh," he said. Then he looked up and saw Tameron. Noah had done so much with the tail over the past two days: training in the Institute of Light, fighting off Charlie and the sasquatches, escaping from a stampede. More and more, the tail was beginning to feel like an extension of himself.

He looked over and saw his parents. He remembered his old self, the person he'd been before the Secret Zoo. A brother, a son. A boy from a world with its own type of magic—love, hope, opportunity. He turned to his friends. They were the best friends he could ever hope for. He'd grown alongside them, creating a special bond and then giving it a name: the Action Scouts.

Noah considered these things for a few seconds more. Then he let the straps slip off his shoulders and the backpack fall to the ground. He handed the equipment back to Tameron, saying, "I guess this belongs to you."

"Yes," Mr. Darby said, "but the courage to use it belongs to you." He started to walk off, adding, "Come! Let us walk you to the door."

Noah smiled, knowing that the door was really the gateway to his kitchen.

The crowd parted and allowed Mr. Darby through. The scouts followed, and so did the Descenders, the Specters, Zak, Tank, and the scouts' animal friends. Noah could already see the gateway to his house, a large curtain hovering above the street.

As the scouts walked, they gazed at the sights, taking in the City of Species for the last time. Metr-APE-olis, the Forest of Flight, Butterfly Nets. Noah saw the Library of the Secret Society and recalled sitting by its indoor fountain, colorful leaves falling from the trees like fairy-tale snowflakes, the scouts listening to Mr. Darby divulge secrets about the Secret Zoo. Then he remembered being in the Room of Reflections, the all-glass area at the top of the library, watching the spectacular video of Marlo flying through Creepy Critters. The Library of the Secret Society—so many memories from one place.

Noah felt a heavy arm drape across his shoulders, and he turned to see Tank. The big man smiled his bright smile and said, "We're gonna miss you, bub."

Noah, feeling like a part of him was already gone, returned Tank's smile and said, "We'll miss you, too, Tank. A bunch."

Jordynn had walked over to Ella and the two were talking. Given enough time, they might have become good friends. But now they'd never have that chance. Zak and Richie were saying good-bye again, and Noah couldn't hear much but an occasional *bro*.

"Here we are," Mr. Darby said. The curtain was an arm's length away, perfectly still now that DeGraff's storm had cleared. Mr. Darby turned to Noah's parents and said, "Might I ask a favor?"

Mr. and Mrs. Nowicki looked at each other skeptically. Then Mrs. Nowicki slowly nodded.

"I have an important piece of business in Clarksville." He held up his hand toward the portal and added, "This is the only way."

Noah's parents looked at each other again, each judging the other's reaction. "What do you need?" Mrs. Nowicki said.

"Just permission to keep the portal up for a few more minutes."

Mrs. Nowicki thought about it. Then she nodded—a bit

238

reluctantly, it seemed.

"Thank you, dear," Mr. Darby said. He turned and stared at his city. He looked at Tank and held his gaze for what seemed like a long time. When Tank nodded, Noah noticed that the big man had tears in his eyes. But before Noah could think about it for long, Mr. Darby abruptly turned and slipped through the portal.

Across the city, the fireworks had stopped, and so had the music. Barely anyone was moving or making a sound. All attention was on the scene in front of the portal to Noah's house. The scouts looked out at the magical sights and all the animals and people who had come to see them off. Blizzard, Podgy, P-Dog, Little Bighorn. The Descenders looked solemn.

"Well," Noah said to Tank, "I guess this is it."

Tank nodded.

The two groups stared at each other for what seemed like eternity. Noah tried to pretend that everything was okay—like this wasn't good-bye forever.

Blizzard took a step forward, and then another. He walked into the open space between the scouts and everyone else and looked up at Noah, his eyes droopy with sadness. Then he swung his head toward the sky and let out a thunderous roar. His cry went on and on, echoing off the nearby buildings and scaring birds out of the trees. Then the mighty polar bear became quiet, leaving the City of Species in complete, startled silence.

Noah felt tears in the corners of his eyes. He lunged forward, wrapped his arms around the polar bear's neck, and held him tight. Blizzard roared a second time, louder than before, and Noah saw more birds escape into the sky.

Very softly, so that no one but the polar bear could hear, Noah said, "I love you, Bliz."

Blizzard sniffed Noah's arms and legs, deeply, as if he didn't want to forget Noah's scent.

"Go," Tank said, and then he quickly wiped away a tear. "Go and remember that the Secret Zoo is safe."

Noah nodded. He released Blizzard and slowly backed away. Then he looked at his friends and said, "Let's go home."

Silence. Footsteps. The familiar touch of velvet.

And then the Secret Zoo was a world away.

CHAPTER 39

THE RETURN OF MR. JACKSON

"Mr. D! Look to your left!"

Mr. Darby and the scouts turned and saw Solana and Evie running up Noah's street beneath the dim glow of a few porch lights. The street was otherwise dark, empty, and quiet. It was shortly before one o'clock in the morning.

Noah glanced over his shoulder and saw his parents watching from the front porch. After panicking about the damage done to their house, they'd permitted Noah and Megan to walk with Mr. Darby to the end of their yard, but no farther. Now Mr. Darby and the scouts were standing by Noah's mailbox—the same mailbox where a cheetah had once greeted Noah at midnight to help start the Secret Zoo adventure.

Evie and Solana ran up and stopped. Solana, breathing hard, said, "Is he really dead?"

Mr. Darby smiled. "He's gone."

"You're sure?"

"His bones turned to dust."

Solana and Evie shared a disbelieving look. Then they lunged forward and traded hugs with Mr. Darby and the scouts.

Evie tapped a finger to her headset and said, "We talked to Hannah. Are we really dealing with Operation Division?"

Mr. Darby frowned and nodded. "The portals to the Outside are already being taken down."

Noah looked at Solana and realized they'd never see each other again. He could tell she was thinking the same thing.

A few seconds passed in silence. Noah glanced at his porch and saw his parents standing by their front door, waiting and watching.

"Mr. Darby?" Solana said.

"Yes?"

"Evie and I worked together this time. Maybe we could do it again."

Mr. Darby raised an eyebrow. "I'm sorry—I don't understand."

"Maybe this isn't the time or place, but I'm asking permission to search for the Specters who went amiss."

"Solana, we've discussed this. The portal is closed. Gone. It can't be—"

"It *can*!" Solana said. "There's a chance, at least. I talked to Zak about this months ago, and he said there might be a way to stand it up again. I'm requesting permission to investigate, and to put together a team of Descenders."

Mr. Darby stared at Solana, and then at Evie. The

scouts waited and watched. "I don't know," he said at last, but there was hesitation in his voice.

"At least let me bring it to Council!" Solana said.

"Council isn't necessary," Mr. Darby said. "I have authorization to make this decision on my own." He looked at Evie, Solana, the scouts, and even at Noah's parents. "If I say yes, Solana, I want you to promise me something."

Solana quickly nodded.

"Promise me you'll work with the others—whoever's in charge—to never let this separation occur again. No matter what. A Specter is a Descender, now and always."

"I promise," Solana said. When she smiled at Evie, the Specter did something Noah had never seen her do. She smiled back.

"And I need you to do one more thing," Mr. Darby said.

"Of course. What is it?"

Mr. Darby began to pull his arms through the sleeves of his jacket.

"Mr. Darby," Solana said, "what are you doing?"

The old man slipped off his jacket and held it out to Solana. "When you inform Council of my decision, please give them this."

Solana stared at the velvet jacket as if it were dangerous to touch.

"Take it," Mr. Darby said, and he shook the jacket a bit. "Take it back with you. To the Secret Zoo."

"Mr. Darby!" Noah said. "What are you *talking* about?"

The old man stepped toward Solana and forced her to take his jacket. "I'm talking about good-bye."

"*Good-bye?*" Noah said. "You can't live without your jacket!"

"Precisely." The old man smiled in a regretful way. When Solana and Evie started to protest, he raised his hand, stopping them. "The Secret Zoo is safe. My work is done." He looked down the street. "It's time to allow myself the privilege of rest. And there's a place I'd like to see. As myself…Mr. Jackson."

The scouts knew what he was referring to. Clarksville Cemetery, the gravesites of his wife and child. Noah had told his friends about the photograph he'd seen in the Institute of Light.

"Mr. Darby," Noah said, "you can't—"

Mr. Darby took off his sunglasses and handed them to Noah. "A keepsake. To remember your adventure."

Noah allowed Mr. Darby to set the glasses in his hand. "Who…who will lead the Secret Zoo?"

"The Secret Council, just as it always has. And Tank will fill my role."

Ella started to protest, and then Megan and Richie. Mr. Darby shook his head and repeatedly waved off their concerns. Then he squatted to get closer to the scouts. "I'm afraid I don't have time for a lengthy farewell. The magic
244

won't last long."

"Mr. Darby!" Megan said with a quiver in her voice. "I don't…I don't want you to *die*!"

The old man turned to Megan and said, "Mr. Darby can't die, child. Mr. Darby's not even real."

Noah studied the looks on his friends' faces and realized they all knew what he meant. Mr. Darby was a character released into a child's daydream.

"You'll keep him alive, I trust." He touched Megan's heart and said, "You'll keep him alive here—all of you will."

Noah felt tears in his eyes. Each of the scouts had them.

Mr. Darby said, "I'd like to sit with my family, as myself, if only for a few minutes."

As Noah wiped away a tear with his sleeve, he watched Ella do the same.

"Come here," the old man said as he waved his hands toward himself. "Come here and hug me."

The scouts dove onto Mr. Darby and wrapped him in their arms. When Noah felt his chest heave, he allowed his tears to come. So did his friends. Mr. Darby stroked the backs of their heads and kissed their cheeks. Then, after more than a minute had passed, he gently pulled himself away and came to his feet.

"The Secret Zoo will always be a part of you," Mr. Darby said. "And I will always be a part of the Secret Zoo."

Memories of Mr. Darby flooded Noah's head. He saw the old man sitting at the fountain in the Library of the Secret Society, formally inviting the scouts to join the Secret Society as Crossers. He saw him dressed in his velvet pajamas for the campover at the Forest of Flight. He saw him catching butterflies, walking among chickadees, riding the Clarksville Zoo train, calling all the animals by name. So many memories in such a short time. It pained Noah to think there would be no new ones.

Mr. Darby was no longer looking directly at the scouts, and Noah realized his sight was already beginning to worsen, the magic leaving his body.

"Go," Noah said. "Before you can't."

The old man frowned. He nodded at Solana and Evie and waved to Noah's parents. Then he brought his attention back to the scouts and said, "Keep an eye on the Clarksville Zoo. For me, and for Frederick."

Mr. Darby turned and began to walk off. The scouts stood on the quiet street and watched the man who'd introduced them to the Secret Zoo fade into the darkness, step by step. The night seemed to slowly cover him. And before long, he was gone.

*

"This is it, then," Evie said.

Noah looked at Evie, Solana, the scouts. The six of them were standing before the long curtain in Noah's kitchen. Noah's parents were by the fridge, still looking shocked and keeping a watchful eye on everything. Solana had already taken down the portal from Noah's closet, and she now had it and Mr. Darby's jacket draped across her arm.

"Yeah," Ella said. "I guess so."

Solana took a small step toward Noah and smiled. Noah's insides hurt. Solana was his first crush, and she was about to leave forever.

"You did awesome," Solana said to Noah. "We couldn't have done it without you."

Noah forced a smile and pretended this mattered. All he really wanted was for Solana to stay, to continue to be a part of his life.

Solana pulled back her long hair, leaned forward, and kissed his cheek. "You're a scout," she said. "Be proud of that."

Noah nodded. "Okay."

"But you would have made a great Descender," Solana added.

He thought of his Descender training at the Institute of Light and all he had learned there—about himself.

"Good-bye, Noah," Solana said.

Noah fought back the tears. Too many good-byes in too short a time. He tried to speak and couldn't. After what seemed forever, he managed to squeak out a good-bye.

Solana turned to Evie and said, "Let's go. You take the curtain."

Evie nodded. Then she stepped through the portal, Solana following. Once the girls had crossed, Evie pulled the curtain to one side, and in Noah's kitchen, the rings clattered along the rod. With the curtain out of the way, a full view into the City of Species was revealed. Hundreds of animals were still gathered, their gazes locked on the portal. The starry night sky was brighter than ever, and countless fireflies dotted it with pulsing light. The City of Species looked like itself again. Noah saw Blizzard, P-Dog, Little Bighorn. Marlo was perched on Sam's shoulder. No one seemed surprised that Mr. Darby hadn't returned, and Noah wondered if they'd expected this.

Evie pulled the curtain, hard. A gold ring broke off the overhead rod and clinked against the kitchen floor. Evie pulled again and a second ring dropped.

Noah took a good look at the Secret Zoo. He studied the buildings, hoping time would never dilute the memories of what they looked like.

Evie pulled again and a third and fourth ring fell from the rod and rolled into the Secret Zoo. She pulled again and took down three more, leaving only two.

Noah felt someone take his hand. Ella. With his other, free hand, he reached over and held Megan's. Then Megan held Richie's. Together, the four friends stared at the Secret

Zoo for what they knew would be the last time.

Evie pulled the curtain again and another ring clattered against the floor. Only one remained.

"Good-bye, Blizzard," Noah softly said.

Blizzard must have read his lips, because the polar bear tipped back his head and roared again, his white fangs glinting beneath the blink of the fireflies. Almost at once, the other animals joined him. Their noise passed through the portal and filled Noah's kitchen—a long, thunderous sound that made the dishes in the cabinets shake. Noah raised his hands, and with them Ella and Megan's, and the four friends stood like Olympic champions on a podium.

In triumph, Tank held up his fist, Sam raised his wings, and the Specters cheered. Then the last ring fell, along with the curtain. There was a flash of light in the place the gateway had been, and then the normal wall appeared.

Silence. The kitchen wall, nothing else. Noah felt like he was staring at the back cover of a closed book.

Ella began to weep, and then so did Megan. Noah fought back tears once again and pictured Solana, Mr. Darby, Blizzard, Sam. He saw the sectors and all the buildings in the City of Species. He remembered crawling across the lily pads in Pollywog Bog, and jumping through colorful swarms of butterflies to get across Butterfly Nets. People, places. Times he would never forget in a world he never could have imagined.

"We did it," Richie said.

Noah smiled. He wondered about Mr. Darby, and if the old man would make it to the gravesite before his body turned to dust. Then he decided that Mr. Darby would—he would because it was the fairy-tale ending to a fairy-tale story.

The scouts traded glances. Then the best friends moved in and embraced one another. Noah felt the warmth of their bodies and the wetness of their tears. It was over. Their Secret Zoo adventure was complete.

CHAPTER 40

A NEW DAY

Noah quietly rose from the couch, careful not to wake Megan and his parents. After taking Ella and Richie home, his family had spent the night talking about the Secret Zoo and all that had happened there. His parents were still having a hard time believing any of it was true. Around five o'clock in the morning, Megan had fallen asleep, her head in her mother's lap. Then Noah's mother, fearing she'd be too worried to ever sleep again, dozed off. Noah and his father had talked a while longer before deciding to close their eyes for a bit. Noah's father had nodded off; Noah hadn't.

Noah looked around and surveyed the damage to his house. The busted walls, the broken furniture, the shattered glass. He saw other reminders of the Secret Society: muddy footprints on the carpet and small clumps of animal hair. He spotted a white feather with a black tip and leaned over to pick it up. Podgy. Noah smiled and gently closed his hand around the feather, deciding it would make the perfect memento of the penguin who had learned to fly.

He walked into the kitchen and looked at the wall where the portal had been. Not a trace of it remained. He waited and watched, a part of him hoping the wall might magically open, allowing him to see his animal friends. He imagined Blizzard walking across the room, his footfalls making the floor quake. Then he pictured the polar bear forcing his snout beneath Noah's hand to let him know he wanted to be petted. Noah felt of pang of sadness as he realized it would never happen again.

He walked upstairs to his bedroom to put Podgy's feather in a safe place. As he closed it inside his dresser drawer, his gaze fell upon his red hunting cap. He paused. Then he picked it up and turned it in his hands.

It's kind of goofy, Solana had said about the cap. *It makes you look like a little kid.*

Noah considered this. He walked to his bedroom window and looked out. He could see the faint silhouettes of houses and trees. It hurt to know that the animals of the Secret Zoo would no longer enter his neighborhood at night. No more monkeys jumping across the rooftops, no more tarsiers perched in the trees.

He looked at the cap, a hundred memories rushing through his head—times in the Secret Zoo, and times long before it. After a few seconds, he lifted his arms and donned the cap. It felt comfortable. Right. But Noah was growing, and he wondered how much longer it would.

He stared out at his neighborhood again. The dark sky was beginning to brighten. And while people were waking from their dreams, Noah suddenly knew that he and his friends never would. Even after his house returned to normal and the evidence of the animals was removed, the scouts would never forget every moment of their time in the Secret Zoo.

Made in the USA
San Bernardino, CA
06 July 2020